HORRIBLY
HAUNTED HOUSES
TRUE GHOST STORIES

BARBARA SMITH

**GHOST
HOUSE**

Ghost House Books

First printed in 2004 10 9 8 7 6 5 4 3 2 1
Printed in Canada

The Publisher: Ghost House Books
Distributed by Lone Pine Publishing

10145 – 81 Avenue
Edmonton, AB T6E 1W9
Canada

1808 B Street NW, Suite 140
Auburn, WA 98001
USA

Website: http://www.ghostbooks.net

Library and Archives Canada Cataloguing in Publication

Smith, Barbara, 1947–
     Horribly haunted houses : true ghost stories / Barbara Smith.

     Includes bibliographical references.
     ISBN 1-894877-54-3
     1. Haunted houses—Juvenile literature.   I. Title.

BF1475.S64 2004   j133.1'22   C2004-903438-3

Editorial Director: Nancy Foulds
Project Editor: Chris Wangler
Production Manager: Gene Longson
Layout and Production: Chia-Jung Chang
Book Design: Curtis Pillipow
Cover Design: Gerry Dotto

Illustrations: Aaron Norell

We acknowledge the financial support of the Government through the Book Publishing Industry Development Progr our publishing activities.

PC: 06

For Sean, Luke, Kyle and Kate
May you always be in good spirits!

TABLE OF CONTENTS

NOTE FROM THE AUTHOR

Haunted houses are pretty creepy, aren't they? Almost every neighborhood has a haunted house. Well, almost every neighborhood has an eerie-looking house that everyone thinks is haunted. Sometimes strange people live in those creepy houses, and sometimes normal people do.

I like to think of myself as a pretty normal person. A few years ago, my house would smell of cigarette smoke, yet no one in the house smoked! We wondered if a ghostly visitor, smoking an invisible cigarette, passed through just to see how we were doing.

And what about the people whose stories are in this book? Their stories might make you wonder about your place. What if you share your room with a phantom? Do you think that would be fun or just way too scary to even think about?

Either way, check quickly under your bed and then read on. Remember, though, that all the accounts in this book are based on true stories! It seems that home is where the haunt is.

Hauntingly yours,
Barbara Smith

TRAILER TALE

The week after his parents separated, Matt's life went seriously downhill. He and his mother, Cindy, moved out of the apartment where the 13-year-old and his parents had always lived and into the first place they could find—a shabby old two-bedroom mobile home in a trailer park. Even though Cindy tried to fix it up, their new home was pretty awful. It seemed to Matt that his life couldn't possibly get any worse.

He was wrong about that. His life was about to get much worse! He would have to share his home with a very active ghost.

His very first night in the trailer, Matt jolted awake. He glanced at his clock; it was 3:23. For just an instant he wondered what had wakened him.

Then he remembered. He had heard someone come into his room. Matt sat up in bed, rubbed his eyes and looked around the small room.

"Mom?" he said quietly, hoping he would hear his mother's voice assuring him that everything was all right. But there was no answer.

Matt tried to tell himself that he was just hearing things. But he wasn't. There was someone in the room. He could hear breathing. It wasn't his.

The next morning, Cindy commented on how tired Matt looked. He didn't want to tell her that something he couldn't see had been in his room. She had enough on her mind right now.

During the day, Matt tried to tell himself that he just wasn't used to the new, strange sounds of the trailer at night. But it didn't work: deep down, Matt knew exactly what he had heard. Someone or something had been in the tiny, dark bedroom with him.

Matt knew that he wasn't going to be able to sleep in his bedroom that night. He told his mother he wanted to fall asleep watching TV in the living room. Unfortunately, just after he fell asleep, he was startled awake by the sound of a telephone ringing.

What the heck? he thought as he jumped from the couch, bumping his shin on the coffee table as he reached for the telephone. He mumbled "Hello" in a groggy voice, but there was no reply. The ringing sound continued. *That sound's not coming from the phone,* the boy thought. *It's coming from my bedroom.* But there was no phone in his room. Matt was wide awake now, his heart pounding hard. He bolted toward his bedroom.

Cindy was standing at the door of her own bedroom, calling Matt's name. Together they went into his room. The ringing stopped. All was quiet—so quiet that Matt could hear those raspy breathing sounds again. He looked at his mother to see if she was also hearing them but she just stared straight ahead and looked confused.

"It isn't really the telephone ringing, Mom. I checked," Matt said quietly.

His mother just nodded. Silently they walked to the living room.

"Let's turn on some lights," Cindy suggested. But the glare from the lamps made strange shadows on the walls, so they turned them off again and waited fearfully in the dark until the sun came up.

Finally, when it was light outside, Matt mother made breakfast. "This is going to be even tougher than we thought it would be," she said sadly.

Matt just nodded.

Through the day, the pair acted as though nothing had happened. They worked together to finish unpacking and hanging pictures. That evening as they sat down to dinner, Matt's mother asked him if he was feeling all right.

"Just tired," he replied.

"You don't look well, Matt," she said quietly.

The boy laughed for the first time in days. "No kidding!" he said loudly. "You don't look so great yourself, you know, Mom. You're as pale as a ghost."

The words were no sooner out of Matt's mouth than heavy footsteps began to echo from the back of the trailer. It sounded as though someone was pacing between the bedrooms. Matt and his mother stared at one another in disbelief. They knew they were the only flesh-and-blood people inside the trailer at that moment. They also knew for certain now that the place was haunted.

When the ghostly noises stopped, Cindy said, "We're going to have to find another place to live, Matt." They both understood that the angry entity did not want their company.

They grabbed their jackets, got into the car and headed for a motel. Anywhere would do, as long as

they were away from the trailer. If the phantom wanted the place so badly, he or she or it could have it.

Several days later, once they'd finally found an apartment, Cindy and Matt drove back to the trailer. They were both nervous as Cindy steered the car into the parking space. Neither of them made a move to get out. They couldn't. They were frozen in fear.

A piercing pair of disembodied eyes stared menacingly at them from the nearest window.

Cindy backed the car up as fast as she could. "Whatever that evil spirit might be, we have to leave it in peace. We can hire a moving company to go in and get our stuff. Maybe the thing will have calmed down by then."

And that is exactly what they did.

Matt and Cindy enjoyed "camping out" in their apartment while they waited for the movers to empty the haunted trailer. By the time summer holidays came around that year, the pair had all but forgotten their horrible nights there.

MUSICAL MANIFESTATIONS

THUNK!——"What the...?" Jeremy exclaimed angrily as his truck crawled to a halt.

He slammed his hand on the steering wheel and fumbled to undo the seat belt. Even with his anger and frustration, he remembered to lift the truck's rusted old hood carefully—the catch didn't have very many more openings or closings left in it. Jeremy certainly didn't need to have that break right now, on top of whatever else had broken down. Peering under the truck's hood, Jeremy soon saw that the fan belt had completely torn apart.

Jeremy sighed and looked up at the sky. It was getting dark. He hadn't planned on this the trip, and there he was, stranded in the middle of nowhere. *Sure hope someone's home at that house I*

12

just passed, he thought as he grimly trudged back along the dusty road and then up to the small, weather-beaten house he had just driven by. He could see lights shining in the windows and music was coming from the little place. He smiled with relief. Maybe this trip wasn't going to take as long as he'd feared. If he could get back on the road again before dark, he could still finish his trip by the next morning.

As he approached the house, Jeremy realized that the front door didn't look as though it had ever been used. He followed the gravel driveway beside the brightly lit house around to the back door. He knocked quietly at first, not wanting to startle whoever was inside. But as he waited for the door to open, Jeremy realized that the music he could hear wasn't from a radio or stereo—it was live music. Musicians were practicing inside! Jeremy knocked again—louder this time.

Seconds later, the door swung open. A small, elderly woman stared up at him.

"Hello, ma'am," Jeremy began. "Sorry to bother you. My truck's broken down and I need to get to Sheldrake as soon as possible. My father's in the hospital there."

He knew he was chattering but didn't seem able to stop himself. "My father's had a heart attack and he's asking for me. Is there anyone here who could help me? If anyone has a spare fan belt, I'd be grateful. I'd be happy to pay for it. That's all I need and I'll be out of your way."

The woman nodded her head and gestured to Jeremy, inviting him inside. The young man could hear the music clearly enough to realize that a fiddle group was practicing Maritime jigs and reels.

The kitchen was warm and softly lit. It smelled like baking. Jeremy surprised himself again by smiling. His gaze fell on a nearby window. It already seemed much darker out there than he thought. *Boy, I really am lucky that this woman's house was so close to where I broke down.*

Handing Jeremy a steaming mug of tea in one hand and a plate of warm sweet rolls in the other, the woman pushed open a swinging door at the opposite end of the kitchen. Jeremy followed her, juggling the welcome gift of food and drink. He found himself in a darker room. *This looks like an old-fashioned parlor,* he thought as he sat down on an old brown sofa.

Jeremy nodded to the musicians, who were too involved in their music to bother nodding back at him. It would be rude to interrupt them to ask about getting some help with his truck, so he just took a welcome sip of tea and sat back on the couch before biting into one of the sweet rolls. Soon he was happily tapping his feet to the music.

The two young women and the young man in front of him looked so much alike that they had to be sisters and brother. The older man was likely their father and seemed to be the leader of the talented little group. As one song ended, they began another. *Must've played together for so long that they know what's next,* Jeremy thought, enjoying the music and the musicians.

The warm tea was soothing and the rolls satisfying. Jeremy laid his head against the back of the couch. He wondered what it would be like to be that close to the people in your family. To Jeremy's surprise, his eyes prickled with tears. He quickly shut them; he couldn't have these strangers see him crying!

As he listened, the sound of the music changed just a bit. The lively tune the group had been playing now gave way to a softer, quieter melody and then to the haunting strains of a gentle lament. Soon Jeremy was fast asleep, dreaming of a day, a dozen years before, when he and his father had hiked across a meadow and up a mountain slope.

Coming awake, Jeremy's first thought was that he felt rested and refreshed. His next thought, though, was that he was cold and uncomfortable. He couldn't have been so rude as to fall asleep on some strangers' couch, could he? Unable to remember exactly what had happened, Jeremy opened his eyes.

What the heck? he wondered groggily. He scrambled to his feet and frantically looked around. It was light outside. He must not only have fallen asleep, but slept through the entire night. Weirder still, the room was empty save for the couch.

Where's the rest of the furniture? My tea mug and the plate? And the people? Where are they? Jeremy thought as he ran for the back door. A few minutes later, he was relieved to be back in his old truck.

Once he had caught his breath from the scare and the sprint, Jeremy tried not to think about what had just happened. Instead, he concentrated on what he needed to do to get the truck fixed. *I hope my old man's all right,* Jeremy thought, not realizing that it was the first time since he'd left home that he'd felt concern about his father rather than himself.

A rumbling sound in the distance interrupted Jeremy's thoughts. A dump truck was coming his way. He jumped out and flagged the driver down.

"Thanks for stopping!" he said.

"No problem, son," the older man replied. "Truck broken down?"

"The fan belt's snapped," Jeremy explained.

"Jump on in and I'll give you a ride into town. Someone there'll be able to help you."

The two rode along in silence and Jeremy soon realized that he had been wise not to try to walk town the night before. He never would have made it before dark.

"Here we are," the driver said, extending his hand to shake Jeremy's. "There's a service station just over there."

"Thanks for picking me up, sir," Jeremy said. "Lots of people would've driven right by."

"Maybe so, maybe so," the older man agreed. "But I didn't, so you just make sure that you always stop to help, too."

Jeremy nodded and jogged across the street to the service station.

"Hello?" he called out and listened to his own voice bounce around the cavernous old garage bay.

"I'll be right there," a muffled voice called from under the hood of a nearby car. "Go wait for me in the office."

"Okay," Jeremy replied and did as he was told. The place was a mess. Yellowed, dusty papers were piled so high they were sliding over. The floor looked as though it hadn't been washed for a decade. A cluster of framed pictures hung on the wall above the cash register. The glass covering the photos was thick with years of dirt and grease. One of the photos was a hockey team and another was an old car, but it was the third one that caught Jeremy's eye.

Those musicians were in that house! Jeremy realized with a start. *And that woman on the end—that's the lady who answered the door and gave me the tea and rolls!*

The young man was still staring in utter bewilderment when an overweight, middle-aged man appeared, wiping his hands on a rag.

"What can I do for you, buddy?" he asked.

Jeremy swung around. He didn't know what to say. He knew he had to ask about the fan belt for his truck, but his mind just wouldn't form those words. Instead, he pointed at the photograph and asked, "Who are those people?"

"That's the McNaughtons. What a great family. Nicest people you'd ever care to meet and the finest musicians this area's ever produced. They played Maritime music—jigs and reels and such. They lived just back down the road apiece," the man explained eyeing Jeremy a bit suspiciously.

"Lived?" Jeremy asked.

"Yeah. They're gone. It's a sad story. The whole lot of them died in a fire at the dancehall about ten years back. The family was completely wiped out. No one even to leave the house to. It's amazing the house is still standing. No one's been near it for years," the man paused.

Silence hung in the air between the two men while the sweet sounds of ghostly music echoed in Jeremy's ears.

CUTTING EDGE HAUNTING

Jennifer and her mother, Mary, knew that they lived in a haunted house. There were phantom footsteps during the night when they were both in bed and the rest of the house was empty. They saw fleeting shadows in corners and often heard a whispery voice calling their names. Neither of them ever suggested moving to another place because they knew exactly who their ghost was. They also knew that he would follow them wherever they went. You see, the ghost was Jennifer's father. Although he had died long before when she was very young, his ghost never let her or her mother forget him.

One morning, as Mary and Jennifer sat eating breakfast, the girl noticed something just a bit different about her mother's appearance.

"Did you get your hair cut yesterday?" she asked.

The older woman laughed and replied with a couple of questions of her own. "When would I have had time yesterday to get my hair cut? What would make you ask something like that?"

Seeing that her mother was not pleased with her question, Jennifer mumbled an apology for having said anything. The two continued spooning cereal into their mouths.

Jennifer left the table first. She was nearly ready to leave for school when she heard her mother scream, "Jennifer! Quick! Come here! My hair! What's happened to my hair?"

The girl raced to her mother and found her standing in front of the bathroom mirror holding the side of her head. Slowly, Mary lowered her hand. There was a big chunk of her hair missing!

"I can't go to work looking like this!" Jennifer's mother wailed. "What am I going to do? Today's the day I'm supposed to have lunch with the new bank manager!"

For a moment Jennifer stared at her mother's hair. There wasn't time to worry about *what* had happened. They simply had to fix the problem—and fast!

"Let me comb your hair," Jennifer offered. "If I do it carefully and put lots of hair spray on, no one should notice."

Mary nodded. Like her daughter, she didn't want to think about what might have happened. Of course, because she lived in a haunted house, Mary knew that there was another possible explanation, but she dared not even think of it. Not right now. Maybe never.

Within a few minutes, Jennifer had skillfully combed and sprayed her mother's hair in place. The chunk of missing hair was now carefully hidden and should stay that way until Mary washed her hair.

That night, Mary seemed to have forgotten all about her hair. Lunch with the bank manager had gone so well that he had asked Mary to go with him to a banquet for the softball team he coached.

The words were no sooner out of Mary's mouth than Jennifer was sure she saw a shadow flit from one corner of the kitchen to the other. She wasn't surprised when, seconds later they both heard the familiar whispery voice that so often haunted their lives. It darted about them like a chill breeze, so fast that if the voice actually said anything, they weren't able to make out the words.

Jennifer and her mother exchanged glances, but didn't say a word. That night neither of them slept well because the sounds of heavy footsteps tromping through their house disturbed them.

On Saturday morning, Mary's screams woke Jennifer from a deep sleep. Her mother had been getting ready for a shower when she'd caught a glimpse of her face in the mirror. She no longer had bangs covering her forehead! They'd been cut off at the roots.

As soon as she saw her mother's hair, Jennifer knew exactly what had happened. The girl shouted, "Dad, I know you're doing this and it has to stop. You're dead now! Mom's alive. Leave her alone!"

For a moment, the words hung suspended in the air. Neither Mary nor Jennifer said another word. They listened as ghostly noises echoed from everywhere and nowhere in their house. Mary collapsed onto the end of Jennifer's bed, put her hands to her face and began to cry.

"It's okay, Mom. You can wear a wig to the dinner tonight. You'll look terrific," Jennifer suggested helpfully, but her mother just shook her head, knowing that she'd be staying home that evening. No date was worth risking the danger of supernatural anger.

Instead of going to the banquet, Mary spent the evening trying to rearrange what was left of her hair into some sort of fashionable style.

For the next few years, the ghost of Jennifer's father made his jealous nature very clear to Mary, and she never again accepted an invitation to go out on a date with a man.

But when Jennifer graduated from high school and went off to college in a nearby town, Mary found that she was awfully lonely. She joined a curling team for single people and began to make new friends. Soon Mary and one of the men began chatting for a while after every game. Some nights, he would take her home. One evening, as Mary was thanking her new friend for the ride, he asked if she might like to have dinner with him the following night. Mary smiled happily and said "yes."

As she said that word, a chill breeze wafted through the car.

The next morning, Mary phoned Jennifer and told her about her plans for the evening. But instead of being excited that her mother was finally going to be getting out and having some fun, Jennifer was worried. She remembered what had happened the last time her mother had tried to date.

"Aren't you worried that Dad will do something awful to your hair?" she asked her mother.

Mary replied, "I really don't think his spirit is around any longer but, just in case it is, I'm going out today to buy a wig!"

Later that day, smiling happily about the fun she was sure to have that evening, Mary drove downtown to a store that sold wigs. She chose one that was very much like her own hairstyle. She came home very pleased. After all, it wasn't every day that a person got the chance to outsmart a ghost!

The next morning, though, when she looked in the mirror, the woman knew she would never wear the hairpiece that she'd so carefully chosen. It wasn't going to be enough. Mary knew as surely as she had ever known anything that she would never, ever be free of her dead husband's jealous ways.

She phoned her new friend and said that she wouldn't be able to have dinner with him again—ever.

She didn't bother phoning her daughter.

Jennifer would find out for herself the following weekend when she came home to the still-haunted house and saw that her mother was bald—and that her eyebrows were shaved off!

ROOFTOP HAUNTING

Judging from the number of stories about haunted houses, maybe having a ghost in a house isn't all that unusual. But having a ghost *on* a house is a bit odd. The following account is about a ghost on the roof of a house in the southern United States. The ghost only appeared on the roof during December and only in the evening. He'd show up the moment the clock ticked off the last second of November 30 and he'd stay until the very second the New Year arrived.

No one knows what the entity did during the day in December, or what he did the rest of the year. No one inside that house knew why the ghost appeared on the roof when he did or why he disappeared when he did. They were certain that he came from a long time ago: he appeared in old-fashioned clothes including spats and a top hat.

It's too bad that people didn't think to talk to Lucy, an elderly lady who lived in the seniors' home. Lucy remembered whose spirit was pacing back and forth along the roof and even why he was there.

Back in December of 1932, a bunch of young men had holed up in that very house. Times were tough then, during the Depression. Few people had a decent place to live, fewer still had jobs and almost no one had enough money. These young fellows had rolled into town on a promise of work, but there was none to be found. What they did find was this empty house.

Young men being what they are—money or no money, jobs or no jobs—they liked to have fun. One night, one fellow found some fancy clothes to dress up in. He went up on the roof and walked back and forth, calling out to his friends on the walkway outside the house. They all enjoyed the stunt—until the lad lost his balance and toppled to his death.

The others left town the next day and were never seen again. But their dead friend's ghost has come back, every December, to offer a permanent reminder that the Dirty Thirties killed a healthy, ambitious young man.

EVIL LIVES HERE

The "thing" that had haunted this house for years was evil. The story of why the house was haunted had long ago been forgotten. The only thing people remembered was that the building had been moved from town onto Ken's family's land, and that it had been haunted by an extremely unpleasant ghost ever since that day.

When Ken was newly married, he often gave his bride little gifts to show her how happy he was to have her sharing his home. Perhaps he knew his home was not a very cozy and inviting place. Unfortunately, the bad-tempered ghost was also anxious to "welcome" Dawn to its home. One day when Ken was away, Dawn stepped out into the back yard for some fresh air. Suddenly, the door behind her slammed closed, locking her out of the house for hours. The long wait gave Dawn lots of time to wonder about living in a haunted house. Perhaps that is what the ghost intended her to do—to think, to wonder, to be afraid.

One night the couple had friends over for a card game. That evening, the four people heard heavy footsteps walking across the floor of a room upstairs. Thinking that someone had broken in, Ken ran up the stairs, ready to tackle the intruder. But as soon as his foot hit the top stair, he realized that the room the sounds had come from was only used for storage. No one could walk across that floor because the room was filled with boxes, wall to wall and floor to ceiling. The invisible force that had caused those heavy phantom footfalls didn't seem to care, although the ghostly hijinks had ruined the card party.

When Dawn brought her cat, Tiger, to her new house, the poor animal had no peace. Tiger would run from room to room as though fleeing from some terrible terror. Sometimes, when he had been sleeping peacefully, he would suddenly jump to his feet. Then, with his fur standing straight out from his body, Tiger would stare at something that was completely invisible to human eyes.

Some of the ghost's pranks were not frightening, just annoying. Like most ghosts, this entity seemed drawn to electric lights and light switches. As a result, Ken and Dawn rarely got a good night's sleep. Most nights, Ken had to get up at least once to turn off the light in their bedroom closet. What bothered him more than the disturbed sleep was that the phantom knew exactly which light would shine directly at his eyes as he slept.

Another time, Dawn watched in horror as a treasured lamp suddenly slid across the living room. Impossibly, the lamp actually gained speed as it moved and stopped only when it smashed against a wall, breaking into tiny pieces.

One day when he was alone in the house, Ken was sure he heard someone fall from the top of the staircase to the bottom. He realized his patience for the nasty presence was nearly at an end when he shouted into the "empty" house, "I hope you hurt yourself!" The hauntings were clearly taking a toll on the man's kind nature. "It was like living in a horror novel," Ken explained.

Ken and Dawn continued living in the awful old house until their son Jay was born. Soon after, they knew that they would have to move. Jay was just a toddler when he sensed that certain parts of the house were not safe. "It's coming for me!" the child would shriek. When his parents asked him what was coming for him, he shivered with fear and whispered, "It looks like poop."

In the spring of that year, the couple began to build a new house. It was on the same property, because they did not want to move away from their farm completely. By summer the little family happily moved into their new home.

Their escape from evil was an enormous relief, though they did wonder what to do about the dreadful old house. Ken hesitated to tear it down for fear of angering whatever presence still resided there. In the end, they decided just to ignore the place and leave it to rot, as any normal structure would do.

Unfortunately, that house was not "normal"—it was paranormal—and it was occupied only by whatever unnatural being "lived" within its walls. Now the evil thing could do as it pleased. And it did.

At night, Ken and Dawn frequently saw lights shining in the abandoned house even though there was no electricity hooked up. During daylight, they could hear the sounds of hammering and sawing coming from it. Neither of them investigated the activity.

Every once in a while they had to enter the horrible old place. The first time Ken went back, it was warm and sunny outside. Inside, it was ice-cold, clammy and dark. Ken desperately wanted to be back outside, before the spirit knew he was there. But he failed. As soon as Ken set foot inside, he heard a heartbreaking noise coming from the basement. It sounded like newborn puppies crying for their mother. Ken knew that there could not really be any puppies in the house. Those mournful sounds were the cruel phantom's way of luring him into the basement. Ken fled to safety as fast as his shaking legs would carry him. The ghostly plan failed.

Others entering the ghost's realm have never found any trace of puppies. Sometimes they found the body of a field mouse or a squirrel that had gotten into, but not out of, the abandoned house. Those little corpses did not rot like they should have. They were mummified.

For years the house remained as clean as it was the day the family had moved out. No spider webs clung to the walls or ceilings. No tumbleweeds of dust gathered in the corners of the rooms. Even the frame of the house stayed strong, not aging or sagging as it should have. Whatever unnatural force resided there seemed to have made time stand still.

This abnormal situation went on until one very cold winter's day when Dawn saw the door to the haunted house fly open. She watched in fear as, for just a second, a blurry, gray, oddly shaped object formed on the porch.

And then it was gone.

"The house is a more natural thing now. It's got bugs, it's rotting and there are live mice, cobwebs and dust inside," Ken explained.

Even so, they won't tear the old house down for fear of disturbing any evil that might linger. Instead, they will let natural, not supernatural, forces cause the house crumble and fall.

RICH AND FAMOUS HAUNT

Near Central Park in New York City stands a big, old apartment building called the Dakota. Some people think the building is so ugly that they call it the "Dracula." Others think it looks elegant and they'd love to live there. Almost everyone agrees that, ugly or elegant, the apartment block is very haunted.

The name of the building might be familiar to you if you knew that a famous Beatle, John Lennon, lived in there until December 8, 1980, when he was shot to death as he was returning home. It is said that, in the case of a sudden death such as Lennon's, his soul may stay on our earthly plane because his life's work is not finished. Such is apparently the case with Lennon. His ghost has been seen sitting at his piano in his old apartment on the seventh floor. Perhaps he is writing even more heavenly music now than he did when he was alive.

Psychics have also seen Lennon's apparition outside the apartment building, especially near the door where he was murdered. Occasionally, he will flash the peace sign at those who've seen his ghostly image.

But John Lennon is not the only ghost in the Dakota. When he was alive, Lennon himself even encountered one of the building's ghosts. One day, late in the 1970s, as the musician stepped into the hall outside his apartment, he suddenly felt that something was somehow different. Lennon paused and thought that he saw a movement in the empty corridor. As he stood quietly, trying to figure out what was happening, Lennon said he heard the sounds of phantom weeping. This sad ghost is well known to people at the Dakota.

Another hallway ghost is the image of a little girl. She has long blonde hair and wears an old-fashioned dress, white stockings and black patent-leather shoes with silver buckles on them. This spectral visitor is always seen bouncing a ball and skipping happily along the corridor, announcing in a sing-song voice that today is her birthday. Although she's a happy ghost, people dread seeing her. It's said that she only appears just before a death occurs in the building.

A couple we'll call the Wilsons live on the third floor of the Dakota. But both Mr. and Mrs. Wilson dread hearing the phantom footsteps that occasionally walk through their place. They know that after a visit from the ghost walker, one or other of them will have an unexpected, and usually quite bizarre, accident in the apartment. For example, chairs have moved as they were about to sit on them, and small rugs have been yanked out from under their feet.

The Wilsons wonder if the spirit once lived in their apartment. One day, as Mr. Wilson was arriving home, he happened to glance up from the street at the windows of his apartment. To his surprise, he saw a large chandelier burning brightly in his dining room. It did not look anything like the light fixture that the Wilsons had in their dining room. Mr. Wilson rushed to his apartment thinking that his wife had bought a new dining room light. She hadn't. The fixture that the Wilsons had installed years ago was still there. And it wasn't turned on.

That night, Mr. Wilson was still upset about the fancy chandelier he'd seen from the sidewalk, and he decided to do some investigating. He pushed the dining room table aside and climbed up on a stepladder until he could easily see tiny details in the ceiling. There, under many coats of paint, was the outline of a type of bracket used to hang a big, heavy chandelier such as the one the man had been positive he'd seen from the street!

Workers decorating another suite in the Dakota were troubled by visits from a couple of spirits. They knew that when the room began to smell musty and stale, they were about to have an unearthly visitor. You see, the strange odor always meant that the ghost of a little boy in old-fashioned clothing was about to appear. The apparition would watch the men for a while and then drift away, becoming less visible with each step he took back to the world beyond.

Those ghostly visits didn't bother the workers. They actually looked forward to the boy's appearances—until he reappeared as a grown-up, but still with his childish face. That strange sighting apparently disturbed all the workers and made them eager to get away from the haunted apartment.

One worker didn't get out of the suite soon enough. As he climbed a ladder to finish painting a spot on the ceiling, the apartment door slammed closed. Seconds later, all the lights went out. He was in the dark—and up a ladder. Then something invisible grabbed the man's arm. Clearly, the phantom had lost patience with the renovations and wanted the workers out of his haunt. The man scampered down from the ladder, gathered up his gear and departed in haste. Not surprisingly, the ghost's hijinks earned it the privacy that it was after, because not one of the workers ever entered the suite again! The new tenants who moved in apparently never complained about ghostly disturbances. Presumably the ghost didn't hold them responsible for the renovations.

Two other spirits who haunt the Dakota are the ghosts of a man called "Joe" and a young woman carrying a flower. They are less frightening—except for the shock people get when they realize that they've just seen a ghost!

Although no one can identify some entities at the Dakota, the ghost in the basement is recognized every time he appears. He is the spirit of a short, bearded man with a big nose and round glasses. He's always dressed in a coat and top hat, the latest style in the 1800s. Immediately after the phantom appears, he removes his top hat with one hand and with the other hand takes off the wig he's wearing under the hat. If that's not strange enough, the odd little ghost has been known to violently shake his wig at whoever has the misfortune to have seen his image. This bizarre specimen from beyond is always recognized as Edward Clark—the man who built the Dakota apartment block. He died in 1832.

Perhaps he stayed behind to scare the people who think his building is ugly and call it the Dracula!

BUGSY'S BOGEY

For a while in the 1940s, a woman named Virginia lived in a grand home in the Beverly Hills section of Los Angeles. The mansion's stately white columns stretched from the beautifully manicured lawns up to the red-slate roof. Every detail of the house was luxurious. Even the windows were huge and grandly rounded at the top.

Indirectly, it was one of those windows that caused this house to become haunted.

In the 1930s and 1940s, criminals often formed mobs. One of the worst of these mobsters was a man nicknamed "Bugsy." Bugsy was as handsome as a movie star and a lot of people thought he was pretty smart. But his actions sometimes told a different story. The last and dumbest of his crimes was to steal money from other criminals! After that, it wasn't just the police who were after Bugsy. The man's fellow criminals were also out to get him.

Bugsy was visiting Virginia in that beautiful mansion with the front columns when the angry bad guys found him. It was all over in about a minute. A car full of the robbers Bugsy had robbed pulled up in front of Virginia's home just as Bugsy was walking past the living room window. The mobsters ran onto the lawn and fired their machine guns at the man in the window. Seconds later, they were gone and Bugsy was dead.

It would be difficult to imagine a more sudden or brutal death. Some people say the spray of bullets was so powerful that one of Bugsy's eyes was knocked right out of his head and clear across the room! Others just said justice had been done.

Virginia moved away from Beverly Hills that very day. Someone else would have to look after the gruesome job of cleaning her boyfriend's blood off the walls and ceiling and floors and maybe looking around for his eye. Virginia wasn't even going to hang around to see who got stuck with the job.

Bugsy, however, apparently stayed behind. At first, no one wanted to live in the house where the murder

had taken place. Psychics who visited the vacant house all came away saying that Bugsy's ghost was there. They said that his death had been so sudden that his spirit was frozen where the hail of bullets had ended his life.

After a few months, most people forgot about the gangster's dramatic murder and that the splendid mansion was haunted. Soon a family with three teenage boys moved into the house. The mother of the family, Martha, always felt especially fond of her family's new home. When people asked her why she liked the house so well, Martha usually just smiled and said that she just felt nice and protected there.

One night, that nice feeling left her—for a moment. Martha had been sleeping soundly when she was startled awake by noises coming from the living room. At first she was frightened by the sounds, but then she decided that one of her sons was up in the middle of the night.

The woman rose from her bed and headed toward the stairs to tell the boy to be quiet and go back to bed. As she was about to take the first step down the stairs, Martha felt someone's breath on her ear. She knew she was alone, but she felt a presence and clearly heard a man's whispery voice tell her, "Don't go downstairs. There are robbers in your house."

Quietly, she turned around and crept back into her bedroom, got into bed and pulled the covers up over her head until the noises downstairs stopped. Only then did she pick up the phone and call the police.

Everyone else in the family felt upset about the robbery. Martha just felt relieved that her life had been saved by her very own special security system— the ghost of a gangster. Maybe because bad guys had killed Bugsy himself, his ghost became a force for good, not evil.

NOW YOU SEE IT

Cheryl knew she shouldn't have stayed at Tracy's Christmas party for so long, but she'd been having such fun with her friends that the hours had just flown past. By the time she said good-bye, brushed the snow off her car and began the drive back to the city, it was well after midnight.

She had only driven a few miles when a strong wind started to blow, whipping the falling snow into a fierce blizzard. Cheryl scolded herself as she drove slowly through blowing snow. She soon realized that she shouldn't be out in this storm. Each minute seemed to take forever as the car crawled forward.

Choking back sobs, Cheryl cried, "I could die out here! Someone help me, please! Someone! Anyone! I'm only 18! Don't let me die! Help!"

With sounds of her own cries echoing eerily around her, Cheryl thought that the wind had let up just a little. Was she imagining it or could she see a bit farther ahead now? Glancing to her right, Cheryl thought she saw a long, low stone fence. Moments later, her car's headlights shone upon a huge, open gate attached to the stone wall. *That must mean a house is nearby,* she reasoned.

As Cheryl drove through the gate, the snow and wind died down even more. She hadn't driven far when she was able to make out the faint outline of a two-story house just ahead. Relief washed over her—she was sure that inside that house she would find someone to help her.

Stopping the car close to the house, Cheryl could see lights on in the upstairs windows of the big old place. *Thank goodness,* she thought. *Whoever lives here is home. They're probably getting ready for bed.*

Cheryl jumped from her car and went up the porch steps to the front door. Her heart thumping, she began to knock on the door, but her heavy mitts muffled the sound. There was no knocker on the door and no doorbell. Pulling off her mitts, Cheryl knocked again and again, but there was no answer.

Once more tears began to fall. She was so close to safety and yet she was still in great danger. Morning was far away and she badly needed shelter. She could freeze to death out there! Drawing in a deep breath Cheryl firmly twisted the doorknob to the right. Slowly, the door opened. She was saved!

"Hello?" Cheryl called out as she stepped into the warmth of the house and closed the door behind her. When no one responded to her call, Cheryl began to make her way up the staircase directly in front of her.

The upstairs lights were on, she reasoned. *I guess no one could hear me because they're up there. Sure hope I don't scare anyone.*

Calling out "Hello! Hello!" the girl went up the staircase. At the top, she froze. Whoever had the lights on must be able to hear her now! What if some madman's hiding and waiting for me? she wondered in a panic.

Gathering her last bit of courage, Cheryl tiptoed toward the room where the light was shining brightly. "Hello! Hello! Hello!" she called again and again but no one answered.

As she went into the room, she told herself that the family who lived in the house must have gone out and left the lights on. The room looked so inviting.

A big, pale blue easy chair was over by the window, and there was a four-poster bed made up with the prettiest bedclothes Cheryl had ever seen. The pale pink comforter looked so soft and inviting that she couldn't help but run her hand over it. As she did, the terror she'd just been through began to slip away. Cheryl realized she was so tired that she couldn't keep her eyes open even a second longer. Shrugging off her coat and kicking off her boots, she climbed between the covers of the bed fully clothed and instantly fell fast asleep.

Hours later, sunlight pouring through the windows of the strange room awakened the young woman. For an instant, she couldn't remember where she was or why she was there. Frightened at first, Cheryl sat up. As she did, memories of the terrifying drive came flooding back. Easing herself from the bed, she realized that she was still alone and that the big old house had been her shelter from the dreadful snowstorm. Amazingly, she felt calm and well rested. She must have had one of the best sleeps of her entire life!

If I leave right now, no one will even know I've been here, the girl thought. She quickly made the bed, pulled on her boots, grabbed her coat and scampered down the stairs. Outside, bright sunlight glinted on the newly fallen snow. It looked like a winter wonderland. With a smile of relief, Cheryl settled herself into her car and backed down the driveway toward the gate and onto the road.

The snowplows must've been along through the night, she noted with thanks.

Cheryl was soon back in her own apartment. *What an adventure,* she thought as she made herself a cup of hot chocolate and called Tracy to let her know that she'd gotten home safely.

Tracy was very glad to hear from her friend. As Cheryl was explaining all the events of the night before—the terrible driving conditions and the welcoming house with the wonderful bed—Tracy became silent. When she finally found her voice, it was weak with confusion and concern.

"You couldn't have stayed at that house, Cheryl. I know exactly the one you mean. I drove past there the other day. There is no house anymore—just a pile of ashes. That place burned to the ground last month."

Then it was Cheryl who couldn't find her voice.

Quietly Tracy spoke again. "I have to come into era and stop at where that house used to be. There's nothing left of it. It's just a pile of burned-out timber and ashes."

Cheryl was bewildered almost beyond speech. She croaked out a few words to Tracy and then the two friends said good-bye.

By sundown on Saturday, Cheryl had seen Tracy's pictures on the computer screen. She had recognized the stone fence and even the driveway leading to the house—the house that was not there. As she stared at her screen she'd finally realized that, on that stormy night, she had been saved by a paranormal encounter. She had spent the night in a phantom house!

HORRORS IN AMITYVILLE

Have you ever watched the scary old movie called Amityville Horror? Lots of houses have ghosts, but not many have ghosts that are quite as nasty as the ones haunting that house! Of course, it's only a scary haunting if you believe that the story is true. The supernatural events occurred such a long time ago that it's almost impossible to know whether to believe the tale or not. Maybe once you've read about the house in Amityville, you'll be able to decide for yourself.

The terrible, unnatural encounters in the stately three-story home began in 1974, when a deranged man named Ronald Defoe murdered his entire family as they slept in the house. When Defoe was arrested for his terrible crime, he told police that the murders were not his fault. He claimed that ghostly voices had ordered him to kill. After hearing that account, people agreed that Ronald Defoe was a very sick and dangerous man. To protect everyone from further harm, he was locked away.

The beautiful big house where the murders had occurred stood empty for a time. Soon, George and Kathleen Lutz and their three children moved into the place. The Lutz family thought that this would be their home for years to come. Sadly, that was not the case. All five of them fled in the middle of the night just four weeks after they had first moved in. During those 28 days in the house, the Lutzes said that they had endured dozens of terrifying paranormal encounters.

Kathleen and George reported that right from the day they moved in, everyone in the family heard heavy phantom footsteps thumping throughout empty parts of the house. Strange pockets of air— either hot or cold—floated about for reasons no one in the family could understand. Windows began cracking even though no one was near them when they broke.

Then the Lutzes began to notice horrible smells. Sometimes the living room would smell so absolutely terrible that no one could stand to be in there. Then, as suddenly as the foul odor had come, it would leave, hideously turning up another day in another room— only the gross stench would be even worse.

Once the smells had started, the house seemed to take on a life of its own. Puke-colored green slime oozed from cracks in the walls and from the ceilings. Black goo dripped from door handles. Nothing the Lutzes did could stop the mess or even clean it.

Then, much to their terrified disgust, swarms of flies, buzzing menacingly, invaded the place—and then flew away, back into the great beyond as mysteriously as they had appeared!

It's hard to believe that anyone could live through such dreadful paranormal events in their home, but the Lutzes swore that they did exactly that.

Unfortunately for the three children, the situation soon got even worse. You see, with each day, their parents were changing into people the kids didn't even recognize! Kathleen's face became twisted and ugly. George grew a beard and took on a look that they'd never seen before. Whatever possessed the house was now also trying to possess the people who had bought it!

When a pair of evil-looking red eyes floated freely about the place, the family knew that they must do something. They contacted a priest who immediately went to the house and tried to bless the place to clear it of the dreadful spirits. But he couldn't perform the blessing. He was driven away by inhuman voices ordering him to leave.

Later that week, the Lutz family realized that they could no longer take the strain of living in such a haunted house. They fled in the middle of the night, vowing never to return.

The Amityville story might have ended then and there except that a writer named Jay Anson heard about this most haunted of houses. He decided to write a book describing all the eerie events the family had endured. Anson had just begun to work on the story when terrible things started to happen to him. Although he'd always been a very healthy person, Anson suddenly had a heart attack. Then his son was in a tragic car accident.

The evil that had possessed the house was spreading.

When Anson tried to contact the priest who had been ordered out of the house, he was told that the man had become very ill shortly after visiting the haunted house, and that he had been moved to another community.

And then a filmmaker—not paying any attention to this terrible run of "bad luck" for anyone associated with the haunted house—foolishly decided the story would make a good movie. That was just as bad an idea as Anson's book had been. Actors hired to play roles in the movie suddenly suffered strange accidents. On the first day of filming, James Brolin, who was playing the role of George Lutz, got trapped in a hotel elevator for over half an hour. The next morning he tripped on a camera cable and sprained his ankle.

A camera operator's car caught fire—even though it was not running and no one was near it. Buildings in which the scripts were kept mysteriously burned to the ground—but the flames never touched the story about the haunting.

Then, once the movie was made and showing in theaters, the people involved in the story began arguing with and even suing each other. The evil spirits in the house would stop at nothing to have people leave them alone. Unfortunately, for a long time, no one was smart enough to be mindful of those angry, ghostly messages.

Eventually, for unknown reasons, the haunting stopped spreading and then died down completely. The house once so filled with horror still stands today, but it is finally a calm place. The family living there claims that now there is nothing unusual about the house.

And that is the end of the Amityville horror story.

There is one other fact that you might be interested in. Long before the haunted house was built, Native Americans living in the area would not go near that piece of land. They said evil spirits were there.

What do you think? Is it too hard to believe that any house could be that haunted? You might be correct, but it's also hard to believe that anyone could make up such a story, isn't it?

SKI SPIRITS

"Come in, come in, come in," the man fussed as he opened the door to the mountain chalet. "Don't let all the heat get away through the doorway. It's freezing out there, but the fire's been going steady in here for a while and you'll warm up in no time."

Kip muttered his thanks, stood his skis up against a spot near the door and walked into the warm log cabin.

"Thank you," Kip said, shivering. "I very nearly got caught in that avalanche a moment ago. You must have heard it, did you?"

"I did hear it. This is avalanche country, for sure. My name's Don, Don Bennett, and I live here. I just love it. It's my little piece of heaven."

"Hi, Don, nice to meet you. I'm Kip. I'm up here with a group from the university. We're on a skiing holiday. I guess I shouldn't have skied away from them, but I got thinking about something in my lab back home and I must've lost track of where we were headed. I'm sure glad you're here. I'll need some help finding my way back to the lodge," Kip told the man who smiled slightly and nodded at a pair of chairs by the fireplace.

The two chatted for a while, mostly about skiing—its dangers and its pleasures. Their conversation wound down naturally and Don stood up. "You get some rest now, Kip. I'll bring in some more firewood."

"Sure you don't want any help?" Kip asked, inwardly hoping that he could just sit where he was, in front of the roaring fire. When he didn't get an answer, the tired skier looked around. *Don must already have gone out,* he thought, a bit puzzled but too relaxed and warm to really care.

Nearly an hour later, Don still hadn't come back in. Kip opened the front door and looked around outside. *That's strange. Don's nowhere to be seen,* Kip thought as he stared onto the blanket of deep, pure white snow in front of him. That's when he noticed that there weren't any tracks, not even the ones he had made just a little while earlier. *What the heck's going on here?*

On the verge of panic, Kip closed the cabin door and looked around. The place was cozy and had everything a mountain ski chalet should have. There was just one big room. The log walls smelled of cedar, and the rafters were open. Snow shoes and animal pelts hung from the walls. A big dining room table took up a lot of the space, but there was still room for a bed in one corner and, of course, the two over-stuffed easy chairs in front of the fireplace.

A newspaper lay open on the dining room table and, not knowing what else to do, Kip sat down to at least read the headlines. A small article toward the bottom of the page caught his eye. The headline read:

Another Skier Lost in Avalanche

Don Bennett, a dentist with a large city practice, is missing and presumed dead after an avalanche swept through the valley where he had been skiing. Experienced searchers working through the daylight hours yesterday found no trace of the man's body. The search has now been called off.

Dr. Bennett leaves a wife and three grown children. "At least he died doing what he loved," commented the man's oldest daughter.

Dead? Why did the newspaper report that Don was dead? Kip thought. *He isn't dead. I just talked to him. He's as alive as I am.*

A few seconds later, the young skier slowly began to understand. He had it backwards. Don wasn't as alive as Kip was. Kip was as dead as Don was. That avalanche hadn't missed him after all.

The newly created ghost smiled. Don hadn't been kidding when he'd said that this chalet was his little piece of heaven! And now, it was Kip's—at least until there was another knock on the door.

Better get that fire built up, Kip thought, as he settled into his afterlife.

NIGHTMARE BECOMES A DREAM

All her life, Evelyn had wanted to live in England. She pictured herself happy and cozy in a little English cottage with a thatched roof. And so, when her children were grown and had left home, Evelyn decided to make her dream come true. She packed all her belongings and left for England.

Evelyn fell in love with the country at once. Neither the gray skies nor the frequent rain discouraged her. But everything was so expensive! Evelyn soon found out that living in a pretty cottage with a thatched roof might not be possible. She was forced to settle for what she could afford—a plain-looking house surrounded by ugly, knotty, half-dead trees.

The first months were difficult for Evelyn. She missed her children far more than she thought she would and, for some reason, she had trouble making friends. Although Evelyn kept asking, no one accepted her invitation to come to her house for tea. Evelyn's dream was turning into a nightmare.

Back in North America, Evelyn's children became concerned. Each letter from their mother sounded sadder and sadder. Finally, her son Jason decided to go to England and check on her.

Evelyn was delighted to see him, but he was horrified by what he saw of his mother. She looked to have aged ten years! Worse, the awful little house his mother was living in was way too creepy for him.

"Mother, come back home with me," Jason said on the second day of his visit. "This place isn't good for you. You're not happy and you don't look well."

Evelyn had to admit her son was correct. Her dream of living in England should have stayed just exactly that—a dream. The very next day, mother and son began the job of packing all of Evelyn's belongings. Late in the afternoon, tired and hungry, the two went to a restaurant in town where they could sit and enjoy dinner.

The waitress recognized Evelyn at once. "You're the lady who moved here from America, aren't you?" she inquired.

Evelyn just nodded.

"I'm surprised that you're still in that house, especially considering what they say about it," the waitress said.

Jason perked up. "And what exactly do they say about the house my mother's living in?"

"Why, they say that the place is evil," the young woman replied.

"Evil?" Jason echoed. "What do you mean? How can a house be evil?"

Her voice shaking a bit, the waitress said, "I've been told that the house is haunted. People say that there is a force possessing the place—it's so terrible that it's twisted the trees that grow around the house, and not even one bird will perch on any of them, let alone build a nest in the gnarly branches. I've also been told that no human should go near the place. Folks around here call it the House of Eternal Evil."

For a moment, no one said a word. Finally, Jason thanked the young woman for her honesty. Evelyn just sat there in stunned silence. That night, as the mists of evening swirled ominously around the ugly little house with its ugly silent trees, Evelyn actually began to feel relieved. At least now she knew what she was dealing with.

Instead of leaving England and her dream, Evelyn asked Jason to stay a few days longer and help her find another place that she could afford—one where she could live in peace. With the help of the waitress and some other townsfolk, Evelyn did find another place.

Today, she still lives near that ugly, haunted house, but her new home is a bright and cheery place. It even has the thatched roof she always dreamed of. Evelyn has lots of new friends who come to call on her for tea, and her children visit her every year. But, best of all, birds nest in the beautiful, majestic trees that grow around the house.

So, after something of a detour along the route, Evelyn's dream of living in an English cottage did come true.

MESSAGE FROM BEYOND

Fourteen-year-old Joy fell asleep as soon as her head hit the pillow. She couldn't remember ever being that tired. Her hockey team had played badly in their last two games and that afternoon the coach had put them through a particularly tough practice. She was sure she'd sleep like a log until morning.

The girl had been asleep for a couple of hours when something suddenly wakened her. She sat bolt upright, her heart pounding. She looked around the darkened room, but couldn't find what might have disturbed her sleep. *Was someone in my room?* Joy thought, giving her head a shake and softly calling out into the pitch-dark room, "Dad, is that you?"

There was no answer.

The girl lay down again and tried to fall back to sleep. Seconds later, she sat back up. What is that weird sound? she wondered, straining her ears. She hoped it was just her imagination, but it sounded as though someone or something very close by had been making strange raspy, scratchy sounds. *I guess it must just be Dad's snoring.* She snuggled down in the bed and put the pillow over her ears to muffle the unpleasant noise.

By morning, Joy had forgotten all about the disagreeable sounds. She wasn't surprised or concerned when her mother reminded her that her father was going to be working out of town for a few days.

That evening, the girl offered to take the dog out for his nightly walk. Rex wagged his tail excitedly as soon as Joy picked up his leash. When they got to the apartment hallway, though, Rex stopped dead in his tracks and began to growl.

"Come on, boy," Joy urged, but the dog would not step forward. She looked around. She couldn't see anything odd—except the way her dog was behaving. "Come on," Joy repeated. Rex just hunched down menacingly, curled his lips back over his teeth and growled even louder.

"The heck with you," she told the dog. "If you're going to act stupid I'm not taking you out. And if you pee on the rug tonight and get in trouble tomorrow morning, it's not my fault. I tried."

With that remark, Joy pulled Rex back into the apartment and took off his leash. For the rest of the evening he growled every once in a while for no reason that Joy could understand.

When the family was getting ready for bed, Joy's mother said something very strange to her. "Try lying on your side tonight—maybe you won't snore so loudly then. You were making so much noise last night that you woke me up."

Joy was puzzled by her mother's remark because no one had ever told her she snored. The girl remembered the strange sounds she'd heard the night before, and thought that if the topic of snoring came up again, she would tell her mother about them. She wished her mother good night and went into her room.

Just a short time later, Joy realized that it was getting awfully cold in the apartment. Shivering, she headed into the living room to see if any windows were open. On her way, she felt something cold brush past her shoulder. A wrenching shudder ran down the girl's back. *That was creepy,* she thought. *It felt like someone just walked past me!* She soon calmed down and decided that she'd only imagined the horrible, cold, brushing sensation.

Instead of closing the windows, I'll just put on warmer pajamas, Joy decided and went back into her room. But, as she climbed back into bed, she suddenly froze in terror. Someone was in the bed with her! She could feel the mattress sag and the dreadful, scratching she had heard the night before was right there beside her. Joy jumped up and ran into the hall, screaming.

"What? What? What on earth is the matter, Joy?" her mother called out as she scrambled to wake up.

"Someone's in my bed!" the girl shrieked. "I felt someone brush past me and go into my room! When I got into bed, there was already someone there."

Sure that her daughter had just had a nightmare, Joy's mother assured the girl that no one could have gotten into the apartment. Her mother even went into Joy's room and patted down the bedcovers. "There's no one here," she said.

Still upset, Joy turned on the light before she climbed back into bed. Everything looked and felt normal, but she decided to sleep with the light on.

For the next few nights, the apartment was quiet. Joy's father came home, Rex enjoyed his walks as much as ever and Joy once again turned the light off when she went to sleep each night.

By the following week, things at school were getting a little strange. Mid-term exams were coming up and some of Joy's friends were acting weird. Three of them even bought a pack of cigarettes to share. Not wanting to act like she didn't belong, Joy took a couple of cigarettes when her friends offered them to her. She told them that she'd smoke them at home in her bedroom.

After dinner that night, Joy remembered that the cigarettes were still in her coat pocket. She couldn't take the chance that her mother might find them, so when her parents were watching TV, she took them up to her room. She wasn't going to smoke them— she didn't even have a lighter or matches. All she wanted to do was hide them so she wouldn't get caught.

By now, Joy was sorry that she'd even brought the dumb cigarettes home. She couldn't think of a good hiding place, and she knew she'd be in big trouble if her parents found them. Finally, her eye fell on a clay pot that she'd made in Grade 4 art class. She remembered being so proud of it when she'd brought it home. She hated to put something as dirty as the cigarettes in it, but it would have to do, at least for now, because her father was calling her to go with him while he walked Rex.

Joy no sooner dropped the white cylinders into the pot than the ornament exploded into a thousand tiny pieces, spreading clay and tobacco and shredded paper all over the floor.

"What was that?" her father called, as Joy tried to stop shaking long enough to collect the debris.

"Nothing important," the girl answered, struggling to keep her voice sounding normal. "Sorry if I startled you. I just knocked something off my shelf. I'll be right there."

Joy could barely manage to chat with her father as they walked Rex around the neighborhood. Bringing home cigarettes had made her feel guilty and then the exploding pot had definitely scared her. What she needed was a few minutes to calm down, but she could hardly have explained that to her father.

When father and daughter returned from their walk with Rex, Joy's mother called out to them from the living room. "I've just been talking to the manager of the building," the woman began. "He said that the woman who lived here before us died a few days ago. Her death was actually a blessing because she had been in terrible pain. She had lung cancer and during the last few days of her life, her breathing was so difficult and ragged that it sounded like fingernails on a blackboard." Joy's mother paused, then added, "The whole thing was really sad because she finally managed to quit smoking a couple of months ago—a habit she'd had since she was a girl. It was too late by then, of course—she was already dying."

"How sad," Joy said weakly. After a moment she said, "I think I'll go to bed early tonight. Good night."

Joy's bedroom was quiet for the rest of the nights she slept there. The scratching sounds never again disturbed her. And although it took a few years, Joy eventually became grateful that the ghost of a woman she had never met in life cared enough in death to offer her a warning from beyond.

CASTLE GHOSTS

Not many people live in castles these days, but years ago lots of wealthy families lived in them. Judging by the number of ghosts in castles that are still standing, those early owners must have been very fond of their homes. Some must have wanted to stay at home forever—even after the walls tumbled down. Berry Pomeroy Castle, in the south of England, is an example of just such a haunted house.

If you visited the castle today you would just see piles of crumbling stone ruins atop a windswept hill. The castle has collapsed, but its ghosts remain.

Centuries ago, a doctor was called in because the lady of the castle was very ill. While there, the doctor saw a beautiful young woman standing on a staircase. He was surprised and later told a servant about the lovely girl he had seen. He asked who the woman was. Instead of answering the doctor, the servant became hysterical.

Once he had calmed down, the servant explained to the doctor that the "person" on the stairs wasn't a person at all. It was one of the castle's ghosts, a ghost that no one ever wanted to see! It was a *crisis apparition*—a ghost that only appears before tragedy is about to strike. The servant was afraid that the lady of the house was going to die, but the doctor assured him that she was already getting better and would be well again in a few days.

A week later, both of them were right. The lady had recovered—but the servant had died.

Legend has it that the castle's harbinger of death is the spirit of a woman who once lived in the castle. She was a cruel person, and as punishment for her cruelty, her spirit was doomed to appear only at times of impending death.

If you dared to get close to the Berry Pomeroy rubble, you might meet the spirit of Margaret de Pomeroy, who haunts the castle dungeon. In life, Margaret was an extraordinarily pretty young woman. Eleanor, Margaret's older sister, wasn't nearly as beautiful. It was their unfortunate lot to fall in

love with the same man. Their arguments became more vicious until Eleanor finally locked Margaret into the dungeon and left her there until she starved.

People who have seen her manifestation report that Margaret is still beautiful, but be on guard if you see her. She is as dangerous as she is attractive. The castle's current caretakers warn visitors that, "on certain nights of the year, the lovely Margaret is said to arise from her entombed dungeon…and walk along the ramparts and beckon to the beholder to come and join her in the dungeon below."

At least three other ghosts can be seen at Berry Pomeroy Castle. The "Blue Lady" wanders about the ruins wearing a blue hooded cape. It is said that she is looking for her baby, who died soon after birth. There also are the spirits of a young man and woman who fell in love, but their families forbid them from being together. In death, the couple is seen forever reaching out to one another, but never quite managing to touch.

These are the tales of the ghosts at Berry Pomeroy Castle—a home so haunted that, centuries after the building itself disappeared, the ghosts remain.

A FAMOUS HAUNT

One of the most famous houses in the world is at 1600 Pennsylvania Avenue in Washington, D.C.— the White House. This stately mansion has been the home of 41 United States presidents since 1800. And it has been haunted for almost all of that time!

John Adams, the second president of the United States, and his wife Abigail, moved into the White House before construction was even finished. Perhaps that is why Abigail's ghost has been seen drifting through closed doors on her way to hang the presidential laundry up to dry in the East Wing!

Dolley Madison, whose husband was the fourth president, returned to the White House nearly 100 years after her death. Dolley's spirit scolded a gardener who was about to dig up rose bushes that she had planted long, long ago when she was First Lady. The gardener wisely agreed to leave Mrs. Madison's treasured flowering bushes where they were. No one has ever tried to rearrange that garden since.

Not far from those roses, the soul of a soldier, dressed in a uniform from the War of 1812 between Britain and the United States, wanders the grounds. Perhaps he's still guarding the house—or maybe the rose bushes!

Two other ghosts also haunt the beautiful lawns around the mansion. In life, both men worked there. They were apparently so devoted to their jobs that they have chosen to stay at work forever.

Even some presidents haunt their former home. In the 1930s, Andrew Jackson, who had been dead for nearly 100 years by then, was heard laughing in the Rose Room. Other people have reported hearing Thomas Jefferson practicing his violin, even though he's been dead since 1826!

President William Harrison only lived in the White House for a month before he died in April 1841. Judging by the ghostly encounters people have had with his presence, it's pretty clear that he managed to hang around the official residence much longer in death than he did in life! Oddly enough, his phantom is most often seen and heard in the White House attic.

The ghost of Abraham Lincoln is the spiritual entity most often encountered. One of the wisest presidents ever elected, he held office from 1861 to 1865. His tall, thin, bearded image usually appears in times of trouble. During World War II, for instance, Queen Wilhelmina of the Netherlands stayed overnight at the White House. At bedtime, the queen heard a knock at her door. Perhaps hoping that someone was bringing her a cup of tea, the woman opened the door. There, before her eyes, stood the image of President Abraham Lincoln! Wilhelmina instantly fainted. Perhaps if he'd brought the cup of tea the queen had expected his ghostly visitation might have been more welcome.

At breakfast the next morning, Queen Wilhelmina told President and Mrs. Roosevelt about her eerie visitor. First Lady Eleanor Roosevelt was not surprised. She had sensed Lincoln's presence herself many times before and also noticed that Fala, their pet dog, would sometimes bark at something that only the animal could see.

When Winston Churchill was prime minister of Britain, he also stayed at the White House overnight.

He asked to be moved to another bedroom after he saw Abraham Lincoln's sad-looking ghost staring out the window of the first room he had been given.

A secretary working in the White House handled her encounter with Lincoln quite calmly. She passed the open door of a bedroom and saw Lincoln's ghost sitting on the bed pulling his boots on. The secretary merely continued with her errand.

Those haunted rooms were renovated in 1952, and Lincoln's spirit has not been seen as often since then. But even today, there are still people who speak in hushed tones when the topic of ghosts in the White House is mentioned.

THE FARMHOUSE
GHOSTS

Danny slipped out of bed as quietly as he could. He didn't want to waken his wife, Jessica. She was still exhausted after moving from their apartment in the city to this beautiful old house in the country. Danny was tired too, but he was so excited to finally be living here that he just couldn't sleep.

Imagine, he thought over and over with a happy little shiver, *this house has been standing on this property since 1783.* It was hard to believe that he and Jessica were actually living in the house. He was still smiling as he made his way toward the kitchen. But when he reached the kitchen doorway, something a lot stronger than a little shiver of excitement went through him.

He was sure he felt a cloud of ice-cold air pass through him. He'd never felt anything like that before. *That felt bad, really bad. It was like someone walked right through me,* Danny thought as he leaned against the wall. Just then he thought he saw a shadow flicker across the room. Telling himself he was tired and just imagining things, he decided to go back to bed.

When he and Jessica finally woke up several hours later, he felt so much better that he didn't bother telling his wife about the strange experience he'd had earlier that morning. The couple spent the day unpacking and settling in.

By 10:00 that night, they were completely worn out again and headed for bed where they slept soundly—until 2:00 AM, when the suffocating smell of smoke jolted them awake. Choking and gagging, the couple fled from the house with only their pajamas on. As they stood on the lawn, gasping for breath and looking back at the house, they were both puzzled. Their room had been almost solid with smoke and yet, as far as either Danny or Jessica could see, there didn't seem to be a fire anywhere in the house.

Nervously, they went back inside. Fearfully at first, and then with more confidence, the pair checked every room in the house. Jessica jumped in fright when she thought she heard a strange cackling laugh, but decided not to say anything to Danny about it. Anyway, she had probably just imagined the unpleasant sound. What was important was that the house was not on fire. In fact, the only smoke in the house was in their bedroom. They spent the rest of the night in the living room. Danny slept uncomfortably on a chair while Jessica curled up on their lumpy couch.

By morning, the smoke had cleared from their bedroom and everything seemed to be back to normal—except that Jessica and Danny were both tired and cranky. And they were both still pretty freaked out about the thick smoke that had driven them from their bedroom in the first place.

Later that morning, Jessica decided that what they needed to cheer the place up was some company. "Let's meet the neighbors and invite them over for coffee this afternoon," she suggested to Danny. "Having visitors for a housewarming celebration should make us feel better. I think maybe we've been spending too much time here alone."

While Jessica was at the neighbor's house extending the invitation, Danny was in the kitchen unpacking boxes. When he first heard the knock at the back door, he was sure that it was just Jessica fooling around. *Two can play this game,* he thought as he pulled open the door and yelled, "BOO!" But Jessica was nowhere to be seen. Worse, a few moments later, she walked in the front door.

For the rest of the day, for some reason, Danny and Jessica seemed just a bit mad at one another. They were both glad when 4:00 came and their neighbors arrived.

After introductions were made and everyone had a steaming hot cup of coffee and a piece of coffee cake, the four of them sat down at the kitchen table. They were all enjoying getting to know one another when first Danny and then Jessica thought they smelled smoke again. Oddly, their guests didn't seem to notice that anything was wrong.

How embarrassing, Jessica thought. *What should we do? We can't just sit here talking like nothing's the matter. If there's a fire in the house we need to get out!*

Just as Jessica was about to shout that everyone should get out, one of the neighbors inquired, "Have you met Nina yet?"

"Nina?" Danny asked.

"Yes, Nina's the ghost here in this house. Didn't anyone tell you that your house is haunted?"

"Haunted?" Jessica asked in an unsteady voice.

"Why, yes," the neighbor answered calmly. "I'm not sure of the details, but there is a legend about Nina still haunting the place. She lived here many years ago. She died here too, in a fire. The flames didn't do much damage, but the smoke in the bedroom was so thick that she couldn't see to get out in time to save her life. She suffocated. They say that her soul has never left the house and that she's haunted anyone who has ever tried to live here."

Danny and Jessica exchanged looks. They didn't know whether to be frightened or relieved. The news they'd just received was both good and bad. The good news was that their house wasn't on fire. The bad news was that they were living in a haunted house.

Later, when their company had left, the young couple talked about the neighbor's story. Jessica decided that she would go into town the next day and see what she could find out. Maybe the townsfolk could give them some idea if they really had bought a haunted house.

The following morning, while Jessica headed out to investigate, Danny stayed home to finish unpacking. As he worked away in the kitchen, he heard a knock at the back door again. This time, thinking that their neighbor was coming to call, Danny opened the door to greet the caller. But there was no one there. Worse, the knocking continued—for hours. By the time Jessica came home from her trip into town, Danny's nerves were completely frayed.

The moment Jessica walked in the door he blurted out, "We need to talk!"

She nodded. "You're right. We sure do need to talk. If you think that Nina is one ghost too many, then we're really in trouble because this house has two ghosts. There's also a ghost outside the house. He won't ever come in—all he ever does is knock on the back door."

Danny collapsed against the kitchen counter.

"Are you all right?" Jessica asked, but she kept telling him about what she'd learned in town. "In the 1950s, a young man riding a motorcycle missed the turn in the road by our gate. He drove straight into the boulder beside the fence. He was injured so badly that there was no hope for him. He managed to crawl up to the back door of this house looking for help. When they found his body, there were blood smears all over the back door. He must have been knocking and knocking on the door, trying to get help but no one came to his rescue. The poor soul's still trying to get help."

As Danny listened to his wife, every bit of color drained from his face. In a quiet, shaky voice, he told Jessica, "We do need to talk."

After they had both calmed down and stopped shaking, Danny and Jessica went out for a walk. They did not want their ghosts to overhear their conversation! They decided that, for the next two weeks, they would try to make their house comfortable and the ghosts feel right at home. If, at the end of those two weeks, the supernatural forces were still upsetting them, then they would pack up again and move back to the city.

Apparently their plan worked, for all of those events took place years ago. Jessica and Danny soon came to thoroughly enjoy living in their spirited home. Jessica recently assured her neighbor, "By now, the ghosts have become part of our family." Then she paused for a moment and added, "Either that, or we've become part of theirs."

A SMALL VISITOR

Jennifer's dollhouse stood in the corner of her bedroom. Even though she hadn't played with it for years and it looked a little out of place, she still enjoyed having it in her room. Jennifer smiled when she looked at the miniature house, remembering the happy times she'd spent playing with it. She would spend hours arranging and rearranging the furniture and moving the tiny dolls from one room to another, always pretending the small plastic figures were real people.

On a hot spring day, Jennifer dashed into her bedroom to change into tennis clothes. Her mind was on getting to the tennis courts quickly, because she and her best friend Tracy had arranged a game of doubles against two of their classmates. If the other girls were as good at the game as they'd been bragging they were, then this was going to be a challenge.

When Jennifer stepped into her bedroom, though, thoughts of friends and tennis flew from her mind. She could hardly believe her eyes. There, kneeling in front of her dollhouse, was a little girl about four years old. The child was dressed in a long, dark skirt with an apron over top of it and a blouse so white that it almost glowed. Her light brown braids were wrapped around her head. *She looks like pictures I've seen of children who lived a hundred years ago,* Jennifer realized in amazement.

Fascinated by the strange image before her, Jennifer could only stand and stare. The little wraith was leaning forward just a bit and happily playing with Jen's beloved dollhouse. The intruder didn't seem to be aware of anything around her. She was having too much fun playing, in exactly the same way that Jennifer herself had years before.

Suddenly, perhaps sensing the teenager's presence, the little wraith turned her head toward Jennifer and the two girls stared at one another across the room and across time. Jennifer gasped. She knew that the scene before her was not from this world. She knew for certain that she was glancing

into the world of the supernatural because, although the child was as clear as could be, Jen could see right through the little girl's image. There could be no question—a ghost—the ghost of a little girl—was playing with Jennifer's dollhouse.

At first, the two gazed at one another in wonder but then, slowly, the image of the little girl began to disappear. It seemed to Jennifer as though the child's apparition had been made of thousands of tiny points of light. The speckles twinkled before fading away. Soon the entire image had disappeared.

Nothing about the ghost scared Jennifer, but it took her a minute to get used to having actually seen a spirit. Slowly, Jennifer began to walk into her room. She sat on the edge of her bed thinking about the amazing experience she'd just had. Her friends and the tennis game were far, far from her mind.

Ever since that day, whenever Jennifer sees her old dollhouse, she smiles about more than just her childhood memories. She never saw the child's illusion again nor was she ever able to puzzle out who the ghost might have been. Still, it made Jennifer happy to know that another child, a child who must have lived long, long ago, had also enjoyed playing with her beloved dollhouse.

AN OLD HAUNT

Even if you don't really want to live in a haunted house, you might want to visit one. If so, Liberty Hall in Frankfort, Kentucky, would be a good choice. The beautiful old house was built in 1796 as the home for John Brown's family. Brown was one of the first senators of the state of Kentucky, and members of his family lived in the huge old place until 1937. Now it's a museum where the public is welcome.

Before you visit, you should probably know something about the haunting at Liberty Hall. The ghost is known as the Gray Lady, and her story is a double tragedy.

It's believed that, in life, this sad soul was Margaret Varick, Mrs. Brown's aunt. In 1817, after the Browns' young daughter died, Margaret traveled more than 800 miles, mostly on horseback, to comfort the little girl's mother. Sadly, the trip was too much for Aunt Margaret and she died just a few days after arriving at Liberty Hall.

Ever since then, people have spoken in hushed tones of seeing a filmy shape, dressed in gray, floating about the mansion. It's probably safe to assume that even though she's been dead for nearly 200 years, Margaret's spirit does not realize that she no longer belongs on this earthly plane. People have seen the Gray Lady busy attending to chores around the house. Sometimes she's seen staring out a window, perhaps taking a break. Even though time has marched by for the outside world, it would seem that everything in the Gray Lady's afterlife has stayed exactly the same.

Perhaps the haunting of Liberty Hall is an eternal one. If so, you'll have plenty of time to visit this haunted house.

SCREAMING SKULLS

Rain pelted down on the motley but determined group of people as they made their way through the muddy streets to the graveyard beside the church. Even the dreadful weather did not prevent them from setting to rest the object that had been tormenting them. This family was on a mission—a mission to bury the screaming skull that had been haunting their house.

Norman Lomas had been the first to see the dreadful skull. He had climbed a ladder to check the rafters of the farmhouse he'd just rented for his family, when the light from his lantern fell upon something odd. It was a human skull! It must have been hidden up in the rafters for years, judging by the dust and cobwebs on it. The poor man nearly fell off the ladder in shock at the sight of the skull's empty eye sockets staring back at him.

Lomas decided not to say anything to his wife or children so as not to upset them. Unfortunately, the skull did not show the same consideration. When the family sat down to dinner that night, the meal was interrupted by a scream so loud that the windows rattled against their frames.

Everyone except Norman jumped up and ran from the house. Norman knew what had made the terrible noise. He also knew that he had accidentally aroused a supernatural force that had probably been dormant for years. It might have lain quiet for years yet to come—had he not awakened it by shining his lantern on the leering skull.

Mrs. Lomas and the children refused to set foot in the house until the skull was gone. So, Norman went up the ladder again, this time to get the skull. He quickly put it into a sack, for it seemed to be grinning ghoulishly at him.

The man took the skull to the barn, where he intended to stow the screaming menace until he could think of something better to do with it. Unfortunately, that move did not solve the problem. The skull may have been in the barn, but the spirit

that had lost its head remained in the house. The horrified family listened as inhuman screams echoed throughout the house all night long.

By morning, every member of the Lomas family was nearly insane from fear and lack of sleep. Norman decided that the only way to stop the haunting was to give the screaming skull a proper burial. Holding the sack firmly in front of him with one hand and a shovel over his shoulder with the other, the man led his family toward the churchyard. As they left the barn, rain began to fall. The closer the little group got to town, the harder the rain fell. Still they trudged on.

Once Norman was inside the churchyard, he looked around, spotted an empty corner in the cemetery and started to dig. His wife and children waited on the street. They were afraid to be near the skull in case it began shrieking again.

As the man dug deeper and deeper into the soggy ground, screams started up again but soon they slowly grew quieter and quieter. Once the small grave was deep enough, Norman shook the ghastly head loose from the sack and let it drop into the ground. Then he quickly covered the hole with earth.

After wiping his dirt-covered hands on the sides of his overalls, Norman Lomas stood by the small grave. Rain dripped from the brim of his hat as he bowed his head and offered a blessing to the partial corpse. "Rest in peace," he said in his most respectful and hopeful voice.

That night, the Lomas family sat together by the fire. The clothes they had worn to the church were hung about the room drying. They said little to one another. Perhaps they felt grateful that their house was no longer haunted and maybe even just a bit sorry for the tortured soul that had haunted their house.

Screaming skulls were once a common type of haunting in England. Just outside Manchester, the home of a family named Downes was haunted by the screaming skull of a monk who had been put to death years before. The family lived with the shrieks and wails until they were renovating and found a wooden box hidden in one of the outside walls. Curious, they pried the box open and, much to their horror, discovered that it contained a skull. Now the family knew at last what supernatural force had been making all that racket over the years. That very day, the Downes family held a small but respectful burial service in a nearby field. And, from then on, they lived happily (and quietly) ever after!

THE HOUSE THAT GHOSTS BUILT

What has 160 rooms, 47 fireplaces, 40 bedrooms, 13 bathrooms, five kitchens, two basements, lots of secret passageways, staircases that lead nowhere and more than 2000 doors—some that open onto blank walls and others that open into thin air? And anywhere up to thousands of ghosts? There is only one correct answer: Winchester Mystery House in San Jose, California.

Sarah Winchester, whose family invented the Winchester rifle in the 1860s, built the enormous home. Sarah believed that her house was haunted by the souls of the people who had been killed by the popular gun. She was sure their ghosts were angry with her and so she tried to hide from the restless spirits by sleeping in a different bedroom every night. She thought that she would be safe during the day, as long as she never finished building the house. As a result, the house was always under construction. The place got bigger every year from 1884 when Sarah bought the land until 1922 when she died. By then the mansion was a huge, confusing maze!

To make extra sure that the supernatural beings did not torment her, Sarah Winchester had her servants bring 13 expensive meals to the dining room table at midnight every night. Then Sarah would ring a bell to invite 12 different ghost-guests to join her. After the meal, the servants would clear the plates (and probably enjoy the food that the ghosts hadn't eaten). Then Sarah would get up from the table and play the piano or the organ for hours so that the ghosts could dance! This strange routine went on for nearly 40 years.

Today, Winchester House is a major attraction for people from all over the world. Ghost hunters have an especially good time—the bizarre building is still very haunted! Most of the ghosts of people killed by the Winchester rifle—if there were any—have moved on by now. It's Sarah's ghost who is very active. Organ music has been heard—even in rooms where no such an instrument existed. Phantom tunes have even been captured by tape recorders!

Sarah's image is said to be so life-like that people think she's a real person dressed in old-fashioned clothing—until she disappears before their eyes! Other times, people can hear either breathing or whispering, but they can't see anyone anywhere near them. Cold drafts and strange balls of light, both signs that a place is haunted, are often felt or seen throughout the house. And Sarah is not alone in the ghostly realm.

The clear image of a man dressed in overalls once turned up in a photograph taken at the house—even though no one other than the photographer was in the room when the picture was taken! No one knows exactly who the man was in life, but he was probably one of the hundreds of workers Sarah hired to build her bizarre mansion.

If you don't get spooked enough during one of the daytime tours, try one of the special night tours. They include lots of eerie areas that people don't normally get to see. After all, it would be a shame to visit the world's largest haunted house without at least saying "hello" to Sarah Winchester's ghost!

HOUSE HAUNTER

When Jackie and Larry Dempster decided to buy a house, they looked for a place that was just a little out of the ordinary, but one that would suit them for many years. The Dempsters were expecting their first baby and so, when they found a 130-year-old house that they could afford, the couple bought it immediately. Perhaps if they'd taken just a little longer to decide about the place, someone might have come forward to warn them that the house they were buying had a tragic history.

Or perhaps not.

After the Dempsters moved into the old place, the ghost only took a few days to make sure that they were aware that they had certainly not bought an ordinary house. They had bought a very haunted one.

Animals are often more aware of the presence of supernatural beings than humans are. Right from the beginning, their dog, who had always been a friendly, quiet animal, began to act up. She would not go into the room Jackie and Larry had chosen for the baby's bedroom. Instead, she would stop at the doorway and growl. Over several moments her growls became louder and more ferocious. Sometimes she seemed almost ready to attack.

Larry and Jackie were confused because they couldn't find anything that might be upsetting the dog. All they could see in the room was the nursery they had prepared for their baby, including more than a dozen colorful, soft stuffed toys for the child to play with when he got older. Larry's favorite of these toys was a teddy bear that sat on its own miniature rocking chair and somehow looked just a bit anxious for the baby to come and keep him company.

What a shame for everyone's sake, even the teddy bear's, that Jackie and Larry had no idea that there was already a child in their baby's room. Only their dog knew about the ghostly presence.

That situation was soon to change.

One evening, as the Dempsters were watching some television, the TV suddenly turned itself off.

Jackie got up and turned it back on. They kept watching their show and tried to ignore the odd thing that had just happened.

The next night the same thing happened, but this time, as the TV turned off, a lamp that had been shining most of the evening suddenly dimmed. The light didn't have a dimmer switch and no one had been near the remote control for the television, so Larry and Jackie were a bit concerned.

"Maybe the house is haunted," Jackie teased, never suspecting that she was actually right.

A few weeks later, little Tyler Dempster was born. The new parents were delighted.

The ghost, however, was not!

One day the couple took their new son out to visit relatives. When they left home, everything was in order—right down to the stuffed animals in their proper spots in Tyler's nursery. By the time the family returned, every toy was in the middle of the floor. There was no chance that they could just have fallen or been blown by the wind—the stuffed animals sat in a perfectly formed circle. It was clear that someone or something had placed them there on purpose.

Leaving Tyler sleeping downstairs, Larry and Jackie picked up the cuddly toys, and put them back

where they belonged. Then they turned out the light and went downstairs. If they were thinking that the strange events were through for the night, they were mistaken. The ghost had other plans.

When the Dempsters reached the bottom of the staircase they realized that the light in the nursery was on again. Not knowing what else to do, they went back upstairs. Before turning off the light, they checked the room. The bear Larry had placed back on its tiny rocking chair less than two minutes before was in the middle of the floor.

By then the Dempsters knew that their house was definitely not an ordinary house. What they didn't know was that they were in for some seriously puzzling and frightening experiences.

Like many parents, Jackie and Larry set up a baby monitor. When they put the baby into his crib, they turned the monitor on before leaving the room. When they went back in to get the baby, they turned it off. Sadly, the monitor did not give them any peace of mind because it would frequently turn off and on—when no one was near it.

Jackie had hung a musical mobile from the top of her son's crib. When they wound the mobile up, Tyler could watch its bright plastic figures dancing above his head and listen to its song. The little fellow loved looking at the toy and Jackie enjoyed watching her son as he lay in his crib, kicking his baby legs, waving his baby arms and making cooing sounds. But Jackie was not so delighted when the mobile began twirling around and playing its little tune when no one had been anywhere near it! Tyler's parents were getting quite concerned about what was going on in their house. Tyler, however, was just about the happiest little baby anyone could ever imagine.

The day that both Jackie and Larry watched a toy suddenly lift up from where it had been on a nursery shelf and hurtle across the room, they knew something serious was wrong. They were even willing to admit that Jackie's joke weeks before about the place being haunted was possibly true. That incident also seemed to be a signal for the phantom's strength to increase.

As Larry lay in bed one night, a hand wearing a black lace glove appeared directly in front of his face. He listened in horror as a voice start to say something. All he could make out was, "I'm going to..." The spirit stopped.

At first he was paralyzed with fear. Then he got up and went into the kitchen to get a drink of juice. When he started to leave the kitchen and go back into the bedroom, he saw the image of a little girl. She was standing in the kitchen staring intently.

In shock, Larry dropped his glass. It shattered on the floor at the very instant that the ghostly image disappeared completely. The next day the memory was still clear enough in Larry's mind that he was able to sketch a picture of the manifestation he had seen.

At that point, the Dempsters knew their imaginations were not to blame for the incidents. They also knew they needed help. Jackie asked a friend who was psychic (very sensitive to detecting supernatural forces in a place) to come to the house. When Jackie showed the woman Larry's drawing, the color dropped from the psychic's face. She told them that she sensed their ghost's name was Sallie and that she was strongly connected to the house.

Torn between fascination and fright, the Dempsters began taking photographs in every room of their house. When the photos were developed, many of them showed strange clouds of mists and other disturbances that had not been visible to them when they'd taken the photos.

Jackie decided that perhaps they could make friends with the spirit. It was nearly Christmas time and so Jackie bought and wrapped a gift for Sallie.

Larry took pictures as Jackie unwrapped the gift for the ghost. When the roll of film was developed it seemed that the ghost had been present for the occasion because a streak of light ran across that picture—but across no others.

Photographs of ghosts are quite rare, but Sallie was definitely not camera-shy. Over the next six months, the spirit appeared in different pictures as a light streak, a mist and a black shadow lingering over Tyler's crib. Once, as Larry snapped a photo, a crayon floated up from the surface it had been lying on and swung back and forth in mid-air!

Larry and Jackie were running out of both courage and patience by now. After all, they had been living in fear for nearly a year. They called in a group of psychics who were very familiar with situations such as the Dempsters' haunted house. The moment these people came into the house, the temperature inside began to drop. A cool breeze blew through each room as the Dempsters showed the psychics around. Thermometers proved that there really were cool spots developing as they moved from room to room, and sensitive microphones picked up strange sounds that the people had not been able to hear.

When the group entered Tyler's nursery, everything seemed fine—for a second. Then, without warning, the readings on the psychics' instruments suddenly changed. Everyone in the room was torn between being very scared and very determined to get to the source of the puzzle. They decided that one of the psychics should spend an entire day and night alone in the house with his sensitive instruments turned on to register any disturbance in the atmosphere. The next day, the man warned the couple that the paranormal force in their house was definitely a ghost and that it was not a friendly entity.

Badly frightened, the family called in a better known psychic. They didn't tell him anything about the house or the incidents. Nevertheless the man, when he walked toward the house for the first time, saw the face of a little girl staring at him from an upstairs window. By the time he had walked into the house and over to the stairs, he knew the image was the ghost of a little girl who had been named Sallie.

Moments later he said, "Sallie is the child who died here in this house many years ago. She died because there was something wrong with her lungs and she could not breathe properly." And then he left.

Larry was determined not to be scared away from the house and to get to the bottom of the puzzle. He began the monotonous job of reading through old newspapers, and it wasn't long before his efforts were rewarded. He discovered an article from the early 1900s that described a doctor who had lived in the house along with a little girl named Sallie.

It seemed that the child had died in 1905; in 1906, the doctor had moved away. Larry phoned the last psychic who had visited their home, and the man was certain that there was a connection between the newspaper story and the bizarre incidents at the Dempster home. The man drove to a nearby cemetery where, in row four west, plot I, he found the grave of Sallie Isabel Hall. Records confirmed that she had lived in the Dempsters' house and that she had died of pneumonia. Although the girl's body was beneath the soil, her spirit was apparently restlessly haunting the house where she had lived.

It's not often that anyone is able to so successfully trace the cause of a haunting. Sadly, this ghost story does not end on a happy note. Even though the Dempsters moved away, Sallie's ghost continued to haunt them no matter where they moved.

NICE AND STINKY

When she first saw it, 11-year-old Katie could hardly believe her eyes. There, on the back porch, was the largest dollhouse she had ever seen! *It's beautiful,* the girl thought as she examined the miniature three-story house. It was not made of plastic like other dollhouses Katie had seen before. This one was made of wood, and inside the little house each window was covered with tiny cloth curtains. Even the rugs in this dollhouse were made from carefully stitched cloth, and the pictures that decorated the walls looked as though they'd been painted by hand.

This is so neat, Katie thought with a big smile. *Someone must have left this for me! I'll set up all the furniture in it and put it in my room as a decoration.*

When Katie's mother saw the new dollhouse, she had quite a different reaction.

"What is that horrible thing, Katie? It's ugly, and whew does it ever smell awful! You're not bringing it in the house! It'll stink up the whole place."

Katie had to admit that a pretty bad smell came from the dollhouse. Maybe if she left the house outside for a day or two, fresh air would fix the problem. Too bad Katie didn't know that haunted houses often have unbearable odors, which no amount of fresh air can ever remove.

But maybe it wouldn't have made any difference anyway—this dollhouse was too inviting. Holding her breath so as not to have to smell the awful smell, Katie began arranging all the little beds against the bedroom walls and the rug on the living room floor.

A few moments later she stood gasping for breath, looking down at the dollhouse. It didn't look nearly as nice to her now as it had when she'd first discovered it. As she stared at the little house, she wondered where the dolls that should have "lived" in the house might be. As soon as she wondered that, a strange voice in her head, one she'd never heard before, wailed one single word.

"DEAD!"

The word sent a jolt through Katie's body. She tried to cry out in fear, but couldn't make a sound. Slowly, shaking with fright, the girl backed away from the dollhouse, down the steps and into the backyard. She took some deep breaths and tried to calm down. She told herself that she'd only imagined the voice and its terrible word.

When her mother called Katie in for lunch, the girl went inside to wash up for lunch. As she sat down at the kitchen table, her mother ordered her to get back up and wash her hands again.

"They're clean," Katie protested.

"Then why do they smell?" her mother replied.

Katie couldn't argue. Her hands did smell really bad—almost as bad as the dollhouse did.

"You can't keep that dollhouse, you know, Katie. It must belong to someone. We'll just have to find out whose it is."

"But if no one else wants it, then can I keep it?" Katie asked.

"We'll see," her mother replied in a way that Katie knew meant "no." After that exchange the pair ate in silence.

By the time she'd eaten her sandwich, Katie was sure that she had imagined the voice earlier. She headed back out to finish setting up the dollhouse. As soon as she was near it again, Katie could smell that awful smell.

Mom's right. This thing really does stink! I think maybe it's even worse now than it was before lunch. I sure hope the fresh air helps fix that, she thought as she crouched down and peered into the little house.

Katie could hardly believe her eyes. Toy furniture was scattered around the dollhouse. Beds were overturned, chairs were lying on their side, tables were upside down, curtains were off the windows and the tiny woven rugs were rolled up and piled in a corner. *This is crazy,* Katie thought. *I arranged the bed and dressers in the biggest bedroom, but now the furniture's all over the place! What happened?* she wondered with a shiver.

Even though butterflies were fluttering about in her stomach, Katie began to arrange the furniture like she had it before. She wondered once more what had happened to the toy people that came with the dollhouse when it was new.

Instantly a strange, scratchy voice from nowhere and everywhere sternly spoke a single word:

"DEAD."

In horror, Katie moved away from the dollhouse but, as she did, she felt a hard push on her shoulder. The force sent her tumbling down the porch steps to the cement walkway below. She landed with a thud.

For a heartbeat, maybe two, Katie wasn't sure whether she was hurt or just startled. Biting her lip, the girl managed not to cry out. She didn't want her mother to run out and blame the accident on the mysterious dollhouse, even though Katie was pretty sure the house and the shove were connected.

And so, as quiet as a mouse, Katie stood up, brushed herself off and went back up the porch stairs. The smell coming from the dollhouse was even stronger now. It was enough to clog her throat and make her eyes water. Worse, not only was the furniture all back in the living room, but a thick, gray mist was swirling around the toy like a small menacing tornado.

That was it. Katie couldn't take any more. She screamed in terror. As her shriek echoed through the air, the mist slowly disappeared.

Katie's mom rushed out to find out what was happening. Some time later, when the youngster had calmed down, the two tried to decide what to do about the evil dollhouse.

Katie's mother's voice was quiet and thoughtful: "We can't give it away. That wouldn't be fair to the person we gave it to. I suppose we could throw it in the garbage," she said.

At first, Katie just shook her head. When she did speak, her voice was shaky. "It might not be safe to leave it for the garbage collector. Let's take it right to the dump ourselves. That way, the thing will be buried before anyone else has a chance to touch it."

And so they loaded the evil dollhouse into the trunk of their car and drove to the dump on the edge of town. In silence they lifted the dollhouse out and together hurled it as far as they could onto the rotting mountain of garbage.

Then, even though it was the worst place in the entire world to wait, they did just exactly that. They waited until the bulldozer working on the stinking mound picked up the dollhouse, dropped it back down and drove over it—twice. Only then did Katie and her mother drive away. Away, they hoped, from their ghastly experience with a haunted dollhouse.

TILL DEATH DO US PART?

To investigate a complicated subject such as ghosts and haunted houses, it would be wise to examine the topic from all angles—even the ghost's.

Have you ever wondered how a ghost might tell a ghost story? How would it feel being a spirit, having a body made of vapor when everyone around you was made of flesh and blood. How would it feel to have absolutely no substance, yet be in a world where everything around you was solid? How would it feel to be part of a world where you see things being done wrongly, but you can't tell people how to do them correctly? Maybe we can't know for certain how that would feel until we're made of vapor ourselves, but after reading so many stories about ghosts and hauntings, surely we can imagine what it might be like.

Let's try.

Let's look at Milly, the spirit who haunts Ernie's house. Ernie and Milly were husband and wife until Milly died. After a few years, Ernie got married again, this time to a woman named Dorothy. Now you might think that hanging around Ernie and his new wife all the time would drive ghostly Milly just about crazy. And you would be entirely correct!

Of course, Milly's spirit drove Dorothy pretty crazy too, and that's why she finally called in a reporter from the local weekly newspaper. On the very day that Ernie and Dorothy told their ghost story to the reporter, their ghost told her story to a phantom friend who haunted a nearby apartment building. The newspaper article went like this:

Local Couple Plagued by Supernatural Events

Ernie and Dorothy Jenkins, well-known citizens of this town, are pleading for anyone with any knowledge of the paranormal to contact them. A haunting in their house has been plaguing them for months.

"It's been awful," Mrs. Jenkins stated. "The whole thing started as soon as Ernie and I got married. From the day I moved into this house there's been nothing but trouble. Ernie thinks that maybe I brought a spirit with me but I think it's his house that's haunted."

When questioned further, Mrs. Jenkins described the difficulties of living with a ghost.

"Most of the trouble is in the kitchen," she told reporters. "Every week when I go grocery shopping I put the groceries away very carefully. The soups go in one cupboard, the cereals in another, but the next morning everything's reversed—the soups are where the cereals should be and cereals are where the soups should be."

The frustrated woman also reports that if she leaves dishes in the sink after dinner they begin to clatter as though someone was stacking and re-stacking them—even though no one is in the kitchen at the time.

"And, at night if we're watching television, the set just switches off at 10:00. That really bothers me because I like to stay up and watch the news before I go to bed."

The Jenkins have had ministers and psychics into the house but no one, so far, has had any luck in chasing the ghost from the premises. If you think you can help this couple bring some peace to their haunted house they would greatly appreciate hearing from you.

On that very same day, Milly told her phantom friend all about everything that had been plaguing her. "Ernie must be even dumber than I thought, and the woman he's married to is even dumber still. It shouldn't take a rocket scientist to figure out that it's me haunting the place. After all, it's my place, too—well, at least it used to be."

Milly went on, "Dorothy's so dumb she can't even figure out that the canned goods belong near the stove and the cereals belong over by the counter. I keep switching them around for her, but as soon as I do, she's putting them back into the wrong spots. And, the lazy woman's always leaving dirty dishes in the sink after dinner. Worse, she doesn't even know how to stack them the right way. Any fool knows that 10:00's a proper bedtime and that the worst thing a person can do before going to bed is to watch the awful news that's on the television these days."

With a sigh, Milly added, "I'm not sure how much more I can take. This haunting could be the death of me!"

It seems it's not always easy being a ghost!

HISTORIC HAUNTING

Sarah lived with her parents, brother and sister in a small Massachusetts town. Their home was over 300 years old and it had been haunted for almost that entire time by the ghost of a witch named Mary. The family enjoyed their little bit of "living" history, but occasionally Mary's antics could become a bit much for Sarah.

Mary's apparition was seen regularly as she floated around the house. She didn't bother anyone; she merely seemed to be living her afterlife completely unaware that it was no longer 1693. But sometimes there were clues that this was no ordinary haunting.

One evening when Sarah was alone in the house, she listened in fear as "someone" angrily slammed every one of the kitchen cupboard doors. Summoning her courage, Sarah went into the kitchen. If Mary was still there, she was not visible. By the time Sarah returned to the living room, the long-dead witch had set a raging fire in the fireplace, and the house became filled with smoke. It took Sarah a while to get the house aired out after that!

It's likely that Sarah's bedroom had at one time been Mary's, because the ghost haunted that room quite often. Fortunately, Sarah came to know when she was about to have an especially extraordinary overnight guest. An oddly shaped, pulsing green light always floated about the house when the witch intended to stay the night.

It's just as well that Sarah was warned, because the wraith could be a pretty big nuisance. Just as Sarah would relax and start to fall off to sleep, "something" would poke at her and wake her up. Sometimes it went on all night. While ghosts don't seem to need sleep, living beings sure do. Sarah was often tired and grumpy the morning after one of Mary's overnight haunts.

Despite the inconveniences involved in living in a house haunted by a witch, this family seemed to have accepted the good (having something really unique about their house) with the bad (having something that unique can be a nuisance once in a while!).

LESSON LEARNED

For 12-year-old Andrea, the worst part of living with a ghost was that she knew she had caused the haunting with her own foolishness. The second worst part was that she'd have to keep what she knew secret.

Andrea had always lived happily with her parents in their perfectly ordinary house. Then one fateful summer evening, the girl did something very foolish. The very next night her carefree life vanished. Fear replaced happiness.

The trouble began innocently enough when Andrea and two girlfriends decided to take a walk in the local cemetery. If the girls had just kept walking, it's unlikely that anything bad would have occurred, but as sometimes happens one thing led to another. Just for a joke, Andrea gave the girl walking next to her a bit of a shove—just enough to put the girl off balance. While she was trying to steady herself, that girl bumped into the third girl, who had been walking nearest to the graves.

"Cut it out!" the third girl yelled as she steadied herself. "You nearly pushed me on top of that grave."

Andrea must have been in a devilish mood because she laughed at her friend and teased, "Scared of the dead, are you?" And then Andrea and her friends began chasing one another around the cemetery.

As they ran, the three girls became less and less careful about where they ran. Soon they were running across graves, jumping over small headstones and hiding behind larger ones. They quickly tired of their racing around, which was fortunate because they were being very disrespectful to the souls of the people buried there.

That night, hours after she'd gone to bed, Andrea awoke from a deep sleep. At first, she wondered what had wakened her. Everything was quiet. Nothing seemed to be wrong. That is, not until her eyes adjusted to the darkness and Andrea could see

the image of an old man sitting in a chair across the room.

The girl gasped and buried her face under the covers. A moment later, as the comfort and warmth of the blankets began to lull Andrea back to sleep, she decided that she hadn't really seen an image at all; she had only dreamt it.

But the next morning, that old man was still sitting in the chair across the room from Andrea's bed. Is he real? Andrea wondered. She rubbed her eyes, blinked several times and shook her head to try to make the image disappear. It didn't work. The strange man just sat there. He didn't move, he didn't even say anything. He just sat there.

His lack of movement is perhaps one reason that Andrea kept thinking she was imagining the intruder. She quickly grabbed her robe from the foot of her bed and put it on before getting out of bed.

Once she was out of her bedroom, the girl felt much more confident. *Wow, that must have been one heck of a realistic dream I had last night,* she thought with a sigh as she wandered into the kitchen to get a bowl of cereal.

But when she was awake, Andrea saw the man again. He still didn't say anything to her but he did kind of float after her in the house for a while. That's what finally made Andrea realize that, even though she couldn't see through him, her bizarre visitor must be a ghost.

For a moment, the girl stood holding her cereal bowl in front of her and staring at the specter. Even though she could feel her heart racing, Andrea tried to be calm. Then, as she tried to compose herself, the image beside her dissolved into nothingness.

That morning at school, Andrea made a point of asking her two girlfriends if everything was well in their lives. Both girls nodded and turned the question around to Andrea who told them she was fine except maybe for having a bit of a guilty conscience about having been running all over those people's graves in the cemetery. Before her friends could respond, the school bell rang and the three girls didn't see each other for the rest of the day.

That night at dinner, Andrea was sure that she saw the ghost walking through the living room as the family ate dinner. She didn't say anything about it to her parents, though. After all, she could hardly tell them, "I think that our house is haunted by a ghost whose grave I disturbed while I was acting like a jerk with my friends."

Later in the evening, Andrea's father asked her to put on a pot of tea. When she lifted the steaming kettle from the stove to pour the water into the teapot, she felt something twist her arm. The boiling water very nearly spilled. As she took a deep breath and steadied her hand, Andrea was sure she saw a human-shaped form floating out of the kitchen.

The girl wondered how much more of this she was going to be able to bear. What was going to be more difficult, she wondered, living with ghosts following her around or telling her parents what she had done? After finishing making the tea, and as she watched an old woman's spirit join the old man's in the hallway to the living room, Andrea knew the answer. She would have to gather her courage and tell her parents that there were ghosts in the house. She would even have to admit that there was no mystery about the haunting. It had been caused by Andrea's foolishness.

But before she had a chance to explain the situation to her parents, the haunting became worse. The family was watching television when Andrea suddenly started to speak in a strange voice. She announced to her parents that she was the daughter of a French doctor and that she had been born in

1851. Needless to say, the strange voice and words coming out of Andrea's mouth terrified her parents. They rushed her to the hospital, but none of the doctors could find anything wrong with her. Andrea herself was now quiet, but she was bewildered about the uncontrollable words that she had spoken.

It's likely that the disturbed spirits enjoyed all the trouble they were causing. By noon the next day, they were appearing to Andrea's mother as well. Perhaps she was angry that the ghosts were tormenting her daughter, because when she saw the man's image she reached out to hit him. He looked solid, but the woman's fist went right through his body as if he wasn't even there.

That was more than enough for Andrea's family. They had no desire to live in a haunted house and so that very afternoon they made plans to move.

Six months later, when Andrea visiting her friends in her old neighborhood, she happened to walk past her old house. It was clear that no one lived there, but something about the place drew Andrea to it all over again. Slowly, she walked toward the house and around to the back door. Oddly, it was open. Andrea walked into the back hall.

At first, she shivered from the unnatural cold that surrounded her. Then she choked. If anyone had been there to hear her, they would have known that this was a serious sounding choke. It came about because two invisible hands had wrapped themselves tightly around Andrea's neck. Seconds later, the phantom hands released the girl and pushed her back out the door into the warmth of the fresh air.

Andrea never told her parents about her last encounter with the ghosts. She also never again showed any kind of foolish disrespect to those who had already passed on through the curtain of time.

LIFESAVING LYDIA

Erin Dawson's family lives in a house that her great-grandfather built when he was a young man. Erin's grandmother and her mother were raised in the house. And now 12-year-old Erin was growing up in the old place. The house was three stories tall and covered with beige stucco. The roof was high and steep. It came to a point at the top that made the house look even bigger than it really was. Despite its size, the Dawson's house was cozy and comfortable.

Erin thought the front door of her house was especially nice. It was bigger than most other front doors and although it was just made of ordinary wood, it was so old that it had turned a deep, dark burgundy color. The door always made Erin feel welcome, and walking through it always made her feel comfortable and very safe.

The thing about Erin's house was that a very unusual ghost also lived there. Lydia was a kind and gentle spirit who'd been in the house right from its earliest days. Lydia mostly kept herself invisible from the living, but on a few occasions she had allowed herself to be seen. People who had seen Lydia did not recognize her image. So, although no one had any idea who the ghost might have been when she was alive, Lydia's job in the afterlife was no mystery—she was there to watch over the Dawsons.

Throughout the generations, Lydia was always the first to comfort any child with a nightmare. Many times when they were children, Erin's grandmother, her mother and even Erin herself had felt the ghost's caring presence beside their beds when they had wakened up frightened in the night. Lydia hovered close by, too, if anyone was ever sick.

The ghost in their house also had a way of warning the Dawsons when news—good or bad—was on its way. The family knew when they heard Lydia walk across the floor upstairs, that soon there would be either a death or a birth.

After all these years of living with the ghost, Lydia had been such an accepted part of the Dawsons' lives that everyone pretty much took the haunting for granted. And that is why Lydia was the farthest thing from anyone's mind one Saturday afternoon in June when Erin and her mother, Pam, were out visiting friends. Erin's father, George, was home doing chores. At least that's what Erin and her mother thought.

They had no way of knowing that he had developed such a painful headache that he'd had to stop and take a nap. They also had no way of knowing that, just before he lay down, he'd started to boil water in the electric kettle for a cup of tea. While waiting for the water to come to a boil, George decided to lie down and rest his eyes for a moment. He fell asleep immediately.

As the man slept, the water boiled—and boiled and boiled—until the kettle was completely empty. Smoke began to fill the house as the plastic parts of the kettle melted. George slept on deeply, unaware that his life was in danger. But something began to disturb the farthest reaches of his mind. He began to hear a woman's voice calling his name, over and over again.

Thinking it was his wife's voice, the man rolled over and groggily called out, "Let me sleep. I have a headache."

But it wasn't Pam calling him. It was Lydia, and she was trying her ghostly best to save his life. Patiently, the phantom kept calling the man's name until finally, with an angry stomp, George stood up. Instantly, he realized that he was in big trouble. He couldn't see a thing through the thick smoke. A second later, George felt a hand on his arm. It was Lydia, there to lead him through the smoke, through the big, old wooden front door to safety.

The firefighters who arrived to put out the blaze told George that he'd been right to flee. The smoke from melting plastic was full of poisonous gases. But George knew that he didn't deserve credit for getting out of the house. He knew that Lydia had saved his life, but he also knew that if he tried to explain that to the firefighters, they would've thought that he was crazy.

From that day on, the Dawsons were even happier that they lived in a haunted house. And every time Erin went in or out of the house, she smiled, thinking that a ghost named Lydia had saved her father's life by leading him out that very door.

THE MOST HAUNTED HOUSE IN ENGLAND

Borley Rectory in southeast England was a gloomy, 23-room, red brick house built in 1863 for Reverend Henry Dawson Ellis Bull, his wife and their 14 children. It was also very haunted. Some people called it "the most haunted house in England."

As soon as they moved in, the reverend and his family began to hear phantom footsteps, strange tapping noises and bells where there weren't any. A phantom coach pulled by phantom horses frequently drove up to the rectory, and even worse, they once saw a coach driven by two headless coachmen. Lights shone in the windows of unoccupied and unlit rooms. Phantom voices called out from everywhere and nowhere in the house. Sudden cold spots and strange odors manifested mysteriously and then disappeared just as mysteriously. Windows smashed even though nothing had hit them. Small objects disappeared. In other words, the rectory easily earned its haunted reputation.

One of the most intriguing entities was the ghost of a nun. Her image was so solid and life-like that when Reverend Bull's daughters first saw her they weren't at all frightened. They were sure she was a living being. It was only after the silent figure had "walked" by them that they realized the image was not walking at all but gliding—just above the ground. A few moments later they also realized that none of them had actually seen any part of human being. They had only seen the nun's habit moving as though there was a human body in it. As the girls continued to stare in amazement, the vision slowly dissolved and then disappeared completely.

The legend of the phantom nun has its haunted tendrils entwined into the time both before and after the existence of Borley Rectory. Townsfolk generally believed that the rectory had been built on the site of a former monastery. According to local legend, the phantom nun was the pitiful soul of a woman who had been bricked into a wall in that monastery—still alive!

When Reverend Henry Bull died his son took over the rectory. Henry must have been reluctant to leave his old house, though, because his ghost haunted the place for many years after his death.

Eventually the reverend's son retired and moved away from the haunted house. For years after that, the rectory stood vacant because the ministers appointed to the Borley Church knew it was haunted and refused to live in it.

Finally, Reverend Lionel Foyster and his wife Marianne agreed to move in. As soon as they did, poltergeist activity began. Keys would fly out of door locks. Horrible smells and strange noises followed the Foysters through the house. Heavy pieces of furniture slid around as though being pushed by a strong, but invisible, force.

As if all of that wasn't hard enough to live with, the poltergeist was about to get much more active. Stones and rocks rained down from the ceilings of whichever room Marianne ran to. Once, when she was alone in a room, she was slapped in the face so hard that the blow left a bruise and blackened her eye. The next terrifying attack nearly suffocated her.

Mysterious messages were scrawled on the walls of various rooms in the rectory; all of them pleaded with Marianne to get help. It was never clear, though, who it was she was to get help for—herself or the rectory's angry spirit.

Finally, after five years of being tormented by paranormal attacks, woman and her husband moved away from the horribly haunted house.

Harry Price, a famous psychic researcher, had heard about the unnatural events in the big old stone home. He decided to move into the place and investigate the haunting. Before he moved away, Price witnessed banging doors, ringing bells, objects moving (and sometimes breaking!), all in empty rooms. He also endured sudden cold or hot spots in the house, apparitions and even a ghostly choir singing beautiful, but supernatural, music!

The last resident of the house was Captain W.H. Gregson. He lived there, apparently undisturbed by paranormal forces, until fire destroyed the building at midnight on February 27, 1939. Some say the fire was started when a book mysteriously flew from a shelf and knocked over a kerosene lamp.

But the haunting didn't end with the fire. In 1951, the phantom nun passed so close by a group of ghost hunters that they even heard her robes rustle as she glided along.

In 1975, a film crew saw ghost lights at the site and their tape recorder picked up "strange noises." Two years later, on a road near the haunted site, paranormal specialist Steven Jenkins and his wife stared in horror as the images of four men suddenly appeared directly in front of their car. The "men" were carrying a coffin. They disappeared as quickly as they had appeared. On their next visit, Mrs. Jenkins took a photograph of her husband. When the film was developed, they discovered images of faces in the surrounding trees.

Even today, people are fascinated by the story of Borley Rectory. One investigator called it "the haunting that refused to go away," and perhaps he was correct. Right after the house burned down, a little boy picked up a brick from the ruins and buried it in his schoolyard.

That school is now widely rumored to be haunted.

SOURCES

The following sources provided direct or indirect inspiration for the stories in this volume.

Adams III, Charles J. *New York City Ghost Stories*. New York: Exeter House Books, 1996.

Blundell, Nigel and Roger Board. *The World's Greatest Ghosts*. London: Octopus Books, 1984.

Emert, Phyllis Raybin. *Frightening Phantoms and Haunted Habitats*. New York: Tom Doherty Associates, 1996.

Fate Magazine, July 2001.

Griffon, T. Wynne. *History of the Occult*. London: Bison Books Ltd., 1991.

Hauntings (Mysteries of the Unknown series). Alexandria: Time-Life Books Inc., 1989.

Hurrell, Karen and Janet Bord. *Ghosts*. Glasgow: HarperCollins, 2000.

Hurwood, Bernhardt J. *Ghosts, Ghouls and Other Horrors*. New York: Scholastic, 1974.

Jones, Richard. *Haunted Britain and Ireland*. London: New Holland Publishers, 2001.

Klein, Victor C. *New Orleans' Ghosts*. Metairie: Lycanthrope Press, 1996.

Jessome, Bill. *Maritime Manifestations and The Ghosts Who Surround Us*. Halifax: Nimbus Publishing, 1999.

Macklin, John. *Collisions with Reality*. New York: Ace Publishing, 1969.

Michaels, Susan. *Sightings*. New York: Fireside Books, 1996.

Myers, Arthur. *Ghosts of the Rich and Famous*. Chicago: Contemporary Books, 1988.

Myers, Arthur. *The Ghostly Register*. Chicago: Contemporary Books, 1986.

Norman, Michael and Beth Scott. *Haunted Heritage*. New York: Tom Doherty and Associates, 2002.

Ogden, Tom. *Complete Idiot's Guide to Ghosts and Hauntings*. Indianapolis: Alpha Books, 1999.

Ogden, Tom. *Idiot's Guide to Ghosts and Hauntings*. Indianapolis: Alpha Books, 1999.

Olson, Eugene. *Strange,* Number 3, 1966.

Smith, Barbara. *Even More Ghost Stories of Alberta*. Edmonton: Lone Pine Publishing, 2001.

Smith, Barbara. *Ghost Stories of California*. Edmonton, Lone Pine Publishing, 2000.

Smith, Susy. *Prominent American Ghosts*. New York: Dell Publishing, 1967.

Spencer, John and Anne. *Encyclopedia of Ghosts and Spirits*. London: Headline Book Publishing, 2001.

Tralins, Robert. *Children of the Supernatural*. New York: Lancer Books, 1969.

USA Today. *I Never Believed in Ghosts Until…, 100 Real-life Encounters*. Chicago: Contemporary Books, 1992.

Winer, Richard and Nancy Osborn Ishmael. *More Haunted Houses*. New York: Bantam Books, 1981.

ACKNOWLEDGMENTS

Sincere thanks to Grant Kennedy, Shane Kennedy, Nancy Foulds, Chris Wangler, Gene Longson, Gerry Dotto, Chia-Jung Chang, Curtis Pillipow, Aaron Norell and everyone at Ghost House Books for continuing to contribute their talents and efforts with to work.

For this book especially, I need to express my heartfelt thanks to my dear friends and fellow authors, Jo-Anne Christensen and Barrie Robinson, whose patience, encouragement and generous gifts of their time and talents scared away the phantoms that occasionally haunted me while I wrote this book.

And Bob, Debbie and Robyn, thank you for being you and for being in my life.

GHOST HOUSE

Ghost House Books

COLLECT THE WHOLE SERIES!

Add to your Ghost House collection with these books full of
fascinating mysteries and terrifying tales.

Animal Phantoms: True Ghost Stories
by Barbara Smith
You'll enjoy these fascinating stories about animal phantoms—some are
scary, others are touching, but all are based on real events. In one tale, a
fish tank with a mysteriously evil phantom terrifies a boy and his family.
In another, a group of foolhardy hikers tease the locals about their super-
stitions—only to be attacked by a flock of ghostly birds of prey...
$6.95USD/$9.95CDN • ISBN 1-894877-52-7 • 5.25" x 7.5" • 144 pages

Ghost Riders: True Ghost Stories of Planes, Trains and Automobiles
by Barbara Smith
You can take this spine-chilling collection of scary stories with you on your
next road trip. Barbara Smith shares eyewitness accounts of encounters
with the unexplained aboard different modes of transportation, including
a mysterious model airplane that provides an eerie warning and a phantom
school bus from the past.
$6.95USD/$9.95CDN • ISBN 1-894877-56-X • 4.25" x 7.5" • 144 pages

Campfire Ghost Stories
by Jo-Anne Christensen
This entertaining collection is sure to raise the hair on the back of your neck.
Read about six glowing orbs of light—the ghostly remains of doomed trav-
elers—that warn campers to leave or face certain death. In another story, a
young girl who grows up with a ghostly double finally discovers the secret
behind her extraordinary doppelganger. And there's much more...
$10.95USD/$14.95CDN • ISBN 1-894877-02-0 • 5.25" x 8.25" • 224 pages

These and many more Ghost House books are available
from your local bookseller or by ordering direct.
U.S. readers call **1-800-518-3541**.
In Canada, call **1-800-661-9017**.